IRONIES

IRONIES

Short Stories from Life

Robert David Martin

ISBN 13: 978-0-578-45044-5

INTRODUCTION

Many of the stories in these pages were inspired by true-life experiences. I was told many of the them as a physician (a psychiatrist) practicing my craft. A few were transferred more or less whole cloth, inspired by the observations of living people. One or two, however, are personal, and they demonstrate fictionalized actual experiences.

I wrote these stories because they were meaningful to me and I wanted to share these thoughts. Some of us compose, some paint, and some write. Those with a creative bent of mind are fortunate. Creativity incases a purpose for living. Communicating with others is a gift bestowed upon some, and it always enriches. We all need something beyond mere mortality to garnish our existence. Otherwise, life stops at the mundane. These tales were written in my creative spirit to share with you.

The last two entries in the book are not exactly stories, though the philosophical dialogue by the prisoner could be viewed as such. The very last is a personal essay which could not be omitted. It remains a tale of resignation which has the author contemplating death. In a way, it's the story of all of us.

Existence is ironic. It's no surprise that the stories about people's lives often include contradictory and parallel realities. Reality is often not what it is perceived to be. Whatever reality we believe, it's important to realize it's an interpretation based on a life learned.

I dedicate this book to my immediate family: Jeffrey, Laura, Linda, Zaylee, Aria, and Barry.

I also wish to thank the people who have shared their tales with me. I hope I've honored them.

Robert David Martin
Great Neck
2019

TABLE OF CONTENTS

A LOVE STORY

Y̲ou want a love story? I will damn well give you a love story. It's not about love or admiration. The usual genders are there. You can't write a love story without genders, but there's just as much hate as love. They're married you know—love and hate.

Mildred was no ordinary female. Then again, what's ordinary, anyway? In the 1950s, "ordinary" was a woman in a pinafore with two children. She stayed home and welcomed the husband. He was a TV personality. Always had on a tie, always smiled, and always complimented her on the food.

You can imagine Mildred did not fit into this. She wasn't a whore either. She was bookish, and she had a hot twat. She knew how to fuck—Mildred did—but that's hardly even applicable to what I'm about to tell you. It's a teaser. There's so little sex in this tale that you can throw it away if that's what you want to read. Throw it away. I don't care. Don't bother with the rest of these words if you want passion, sex, spread legs, men with their members pointing to the ceiling, and the like. If you want a tale of psychological oddity and a life in a symbol, read on.

Mildred loved no one. She was a miserable woman—a depressive, I believe. At least, that's what Simon told me. He hated her. After thirty-six years, he couldn't stand her. He thought she was a pompous snob. She read books; he fixed cars. There was no connection between them. They weren't married; they never had sex. Simon knew her, but she didn't know him. At least she didn't know him when he told me she was a bitch and spat on the ground. They later met because of a dog.

Mildred's dog lived on the same block as Simon who was married to Sarah. They were a Jewish couple. Mildred was Jewish and Irish, but mostly Jewish. It was a block of walk-ups with little porches at the top of the stairs where no one ever sat. The snow tended to stay on the steps and porch in the winter, and sometimes the dog shit remained on Mildred's entrance, though mostly cleaned. When she took care of the excrement, she did it well, with only occasional slips.

At some point, as you will see, Mildred's dog bit Sarah.

Sarah and Simon had been living on the same block as Mildred for thirty-six years, and they grew to hate her, even though they had never met her. They lived at the opposite end of the block, and the street was situated such that Mildred could easily have avoided walking by their house. But she didn't. Every Saturday, and only on Saturday, she took the most unlikely route—sauntering along the sidewalk just in front of the Netherlanders' home, far away from her usual walk. For years, she wasn't noticed, but one day Sarah was about to step out the door when she spied Mildred pausing, with her dog, right in front of her house. She didn't feel any hate at that time. She just felt puzzled. Why was this woman pausing in front of her doorway? That was over twenty years ago. Like the sprinkling inflicted by drip-drop inflicted by the water torture of a Second World War Japanese prisoner, Sarah began to be more and more bothered every Saturday. Mildred was nowhere to be seen every other day, Monday, Tuesday, Wednesday, Thursday, Friday, or Sunday—only on Saturday. For twenty years, every Saturday, Mildred walked her damn dog down the sidewalk before the Netherlanders', and she thought nothing of it.

Sarah thought about it a lot. She began to talk to Simon about this woman they didn't know. They waited for her on the expected day. Mildred changed the time of her regular schedule, but only within an hour or so. She always made her provocation before noon.

"Why does that damn woman walk her dog in front of our house every Saturday?" Sarah queried Simon passionately.

"Forget about it," he replied. He was too Jewish. He was more concerned about Palestinian uprisings and Yom Kippur than a woman and her ambulation's. Mildred was Jewish too (well, part anyway), but her ethnicity was simply of no concern.

One day the Netherlanders received a wedding invitation from Sarah's brother. At the jaunty age of forty-two, he was getting married. The name of the bride on the invitation was Mildred Kanter. They both wondered if it could possibly be the name of the woman with the dog.

"Do you think it's the name of the same damn woman with that damn fucking dog?" Sarah asked.

"I don't know. Why don't you call your brother and ask him?"

She did. It was.

The day came when they were all to meet. Sarah's brother was giving a party at his house, a small affair with about twenty-five people. The Netherlanders brought a gift, feeling it was necessary. Sarah wasn't close to her brother, and she didn't particularly love him, but she didn't want strife where it wasn't necessary. She also argued to herself that Mildred was an unknown. Just because she walked in front of the house every Saturday for decades didn't mean she was an intolerable rat. Simon was indifferent. To him, the entire dog story was a woman's nightmare of which he wanted no part. However, matters were about to change.

They had no trouble finding Mildred. She was without the dog, but she looked exactly as expected—except for the flowery spring dress inappropriate for this cold winter day. Sarah tried to strike up a conversation. Mildred was delighted. The two women hit it off immediately. In fact, they fell in love. It must be mentioned again, of course, that day, there was no dog.

So, Mildred married George, Sarah's brother, but became Sarah's surreptitious lover. George and Simon didn't have a clue. It never occurred to Simon to suspect the mother of his children to be a lesbian. George had a good sex life with Mildred that he never considered that he was insufficient as a lover. All of this continued for a while—until the dog bite.

It turned out George's apartment was up for a lease renewal, and Mildred's house—left to her by two feuding parents, who died together in a Long Island Expressway auto crash—was a better place to live anyway. He moved in. They had a daughter who was much too young to realize that her mother was in a homosexual relationship with the frequent visitor.

All went on in this unlikely manner for longer than you'd think. Like all love affairs, this one had its denouement. Mildred began to tire of Sarah. Besides, Sarah could not hide the fact that she hated Mildred's mutt. It was always yapping at her and peeing on the porch of her house when Mildred and George happened to visit, making a cursed nuisance of itself. Mildred deeply loved the dog but hated Sarah's attitude. Slowly, her resentment interfered with the sex. She just wasn't into it anymore. Sarah felt the rejection.

Just as they were breaking up, but before they announced it to each other, Sarah came over for one of her secret visits. As she marched up the eight steps, she saw the mutt on the porch and Mildred behind the window. For the first time, she paused, feeling the personal animosity of this animal. It snarled, and before she could maneuver, it jumped and bit a piece out of her ankle.

This and Mildred's rejection, which followed much too soon after, were too much. Even though her secret mate tried to make amends (putting on a bandage, saying how sorry she was, and so forth), Sarah could not hide her frustration, her bereavement at the loss of a fantasized perfect love, and the burning realization that she would now be left for the rest of her life to the sexual machinations of her sexually untalented husband.

She sued.

Mildred was thrown in jail for thirty-six hours. She was ultimately fined $10,000 for injuries caused by the little beast, and the court dictated that she had to put it to sleep.

Love turned to hate. Real hate. Credit must be given to Mildred. She could have caused serious harm by revealing the lesbian relationship, but she didn't. She and Sarah never revealed what would have destroyed both their marriages. Sarah held a strange sense of gratitude toward her ex-lover, but the hate persisted.

Mildred got a new dog, and every Sunday, it shat upon the Netherlanders' front porch. There was no way to prove it. Mildred's daughter was a brat, and she played a trumpet in front of the Netherlanders' home every day while going to school. Surely, Mildred put her up to it. Sarah couldn't fathom the mystery of why no other neighbor complained, but it drove her crazy. Occasionally, Mildred would park her car in front of the Netherlander's house, even though her house was at the extreme end of the block. It was a perfectly legal spot, and there was no way to complain. Sarah would tremble with rage. One day, on impulse, Sarah sprayed paint on the blue car's trunk. The white paint screamed out. It was all too obvious. Someone had done this on purpose. Who?

Life went on with tits for tats until Mildred developed kidney cancer and died at the age of fifty-two. Sarah did not go to the funeral. She heard that George cried. Simon was happy it was finally all over. Mildred and Sarah's secret nearly had its own funeral, except for one little note found in Mildred's panty drawer while her daughter was looking for a beret. She showed the crumpled paper to her father. It was Mildred's note to herself. It simply read, "I hate that lesbian."

No one knew what she meant.

SWANN'S WAY

SWANN: This is not a new problem. I've had it for years. It just seems to have gotten worse.

DOCTOR: What do you think is making it worse?

SWANN: I think it has something to do with maturity. For a long time, I just accepted it. I don't think I really knew it was a symptom or a problem—you know what I mean? It just seemed like me. But now that I've turned "that age," it hit me that it was not right. I mean I think it's time I did something about it.

DOCTOR: So, for the first time, you recognized your inclination toward ducks as a symptom, something abnormal, and you want to do something about it?

SWANN: Yes.

DOCTOR: You want to eliminate this inclination?

SWANN: Definitely. After all, I am a swan. I am not a duck. It just doesn't make sense that I want to be with ducks all the time. Of course, I fight it. No other swan knows what I go through. I am pretty good at keeping it to myself, but it affects me. With others, I often find myself too quiet. Afterward, I feel I missed an opportunity to make friends. I know there is something wrong, and it has to do with this duck thing, but I can't quite put it all together.

DOCTOR: I understand. One way to approach this is to obtain an understanding of your background. Tell me a little more about yourself. What important things can you remember about your past? Does anything you can remember seem relevant to the problem about ducks?

SWANN: Ducks? Ducks? My God! Yes! Why didn't I think of that before? I am so stupid. It's so obvious. What's the matter with me?

DOCTOR: There is nothing fundamentally wrong with you. You are really quite a normal swan with a particular problem. It often happens that problems in the past escape our recall and affect our lives outside of our awareness. Just relax and tell me what you remember that might be important.

SWANN: Doctor, please don't think I'm foolish for not considering this before. It's all so clear now.

DOCTOR: Of course. Now tell me about it.

SWANN: Don't be surprised, Doctor, but I was brought up by ducks.

DOCTOR: Your parents were ducks? Impossible! How can that be?

SWANN: I was not really born from ducks. I was brought up by them.

DOCTOR: Oh. Go on.

SWANN: Well...I don't know what happened to my real parents. I don't think anyone knows. All I can remember is that when I first awoke to the light of day, I was with ducks my own age.

DOCTOR: How did you feel about this? It must have been unsettling to know you were with ducks and not baby swans?

SWANN: That's just it. I didn't know. I thought I was the same as
they were. I thought I was a duck.

DOCTOR: I see. Very interesting.

SWANN: That was not the worst part of it. My brothers and sisters, or at least the ducks I believed were my brothers
and sisters, noticed that I was different. They immediately began avoiding me and always put me at the end
of the line. When I sometimes had trouble keeping up,
they yelled at me and called me names.

DOCTOR: Do you remember any of these names?

SWANN: One sticks in my mind. I think I will never forget it
now, thanks to you.

DOCTOR: Yes?

SWANN: "Ugly"! That's it. Yes, they always called me the "ugly
duckling."

DOCTOR: That must have been very upsetting.

SWANN: It was. I was mortified. I didn't know what to do. I cried
to myself, and I always made sure they didn't see me so
upset. I thought they would pick on me more if they
knew. What's worse is I believed them. When I looked
into a pool of water, I saw that I was very different. I
didn't look like the rest of them at all. I truly believed
that I was a duck and that I was ugly.

DOCTOR: Well! Didn't your adoptive parents do anything to help?
Didn't they recognize that you were not a duck, try to
find your real parents, or protect you from your adoptive siblings?

SWANN: No, nothing. They ignored the whole thing. All they
did was swim about in the pond as if nothing was going
on. I think they knew I was around, but they acted as if

they didn't. Looking back, I don't think they wanted to face up to the full meaning of my presence.

DOCTOR: Why do you think so? Any ideas?

SWANN: Yes. It all seems so clear now. If they recognized the problem, they would have had to explain my presence. I don't know if they had any part to play in my being in their litter. Perhaps yes, perhaps no. If so, their guilt would be obvious. In any case they would have had to tell their own ducklings. Then it would have been necessary for them to deal with the conflicts between them and me. You see, my parents were quiet ducks. They avoided problems altogether. I really can't understand why they had ducklings at all. They would have been just as happy flying south in the winter and north in the summer without the added worries of a family. It wasn't just that I was too much to deal with. Everything was too much to deal with. They were simple ducks without much sophistication. They couldn't handle a duckling that was really a swan. So they denied it.

DOCTOR: Hmm. Good. Go on.

SWANN: They were not all bad. My duck parents saw to it that I was fed. I was never neglected as far as my basic needs were concerned. Despite their psychological blindness, they were good parents when it came to the necessities. I...I...I can't believe I'm crying. It's wonderful. I haven't cried in years. Real tears! It's true. I do love them. But I'm angry at them too. Why didn't they understand what I was going through? Sure, they didn't reject me, but they sure as hell didn't get involved in my emotional needs either.

DOCTOR: So, if I understand you, your inclination to be with ducks comes from this early experience. You were, as a child, a duckling, so to speak. Upon growing up, your transformation into a swan went very far into helping you overcome your antipathy toward yourself as an ugly duckling but never removed the feeling that there was something wrong with you. The conflict was so great in your subconscious that you suppressed your past, lived as a swan, but never felt right about it. All of this was complicated by your ambivalent relationship with your adoptive parents. You loved and hated them. Your memories, only vaguely remembered but mostly in your subconscious, drew you both toward and away from the members of your family. These conflicts made you want to be with ducks and, simultaneously, stay away from them to sustain your own true identity. Realizing that your original swan parents rejected you complicated the problem of accepting yourself as a swan. It must have been very difficult for you, all this?

SWANN: It was! It was! This is all so wonderful! I'm so grateful to you, Doctor. I would have never figured all this out by myself. Thank you.

DOCTOR: Do not thank me. You did the work. I have only been your guide. We must now see if the symptom disappears.

SWANN: I may be wrong, but I think it will. I realize that what happened to me was an accident of nature. I hold no one to blame. I feel I understand it all.

DOCTOR: I think you understand a great deal, but we are not through. Do not be impatient. There is still more to do.

SWANN: We are not through?

DOCTOR: No. We have just begun.

PHO BAC

"Do you want to hear this story now or wait for our soup?"
"Whichever you prefer. You can start now if you want. It's incredible, you say?"

"Yeah, really—simple in detail, but incredible in overall effect. Your ordering soup made me think of it. The experience was unexpected, weird. When was the last time a Vietnamese guy spoke to you spontaneously? Never, I'll bet."

"Never, you're right. I think I'm just too Caucasian for such cultural crossovers. Soup? It begs a metaphor."

"Spare me. So as I said, this guy is from Vietnam."

"I'm listening. So how did you meet him?"

"I didn't, really. He was sitting alone at a restaurant table. I was alone too, having lunch by myself. I only had an hour. (The place is near my office.) What was it that happened? Ah, yes, the waiter brought us the same dish and remarked at my good taste. I told him I just picked it from the picture. It was some kind of fish recipe, with spicy soup with exotic fruits, ginger and noodles. The Vietnamese guy said this was a famous dish in Vietnam, and we got talking. After a while, he asked me if I wanted to join him. It seemed like an interesting offer, so I moved over to sit with him. He seemed to want to talk, and the next thing I knew, he asked if I wanted to hear an incredible tale. I had the time and, of course, I said yes.

"I know little about the Vietnamese culture. I can only relate what he told me. The aligning events are so unlikely. Chaos theory or complexity theory comes to mind. So many unlikely variables coming together to create an unlikely happening…well, let me get on with it.

"I never learned his real name, but he was called 'Soup.' Of course, in Vietnamese, the name is different: Pho Bac. His mother was a prostitute during the war. One of her Johns was an American lieutenant colonel named Stringe. Pho Bac was born from a union between these two. He said he was certain of this and that he even has a US-stamped paper to certify that Lieutenant Colonel Stringe is, indeed, his father. He's neither sure if he ever saw his father nor if his mother was a prostitute when he was conceived. His earliest memory was his bringing soup to the women who worked with his mother. He thinks he was, perhaps, five. This is where he got his name. Instead of calling him by his given name, the women came to call him Pho Bac.

"His life was sordid and miserable, but he hardly knew this at the time of his childhood. He knew his father was an American officer, but only that he had disappeared. His mother used to tell him that one day the officer would return, that he had promised her he would return, and that until then they had to survive. He felt delivering soup and getting the small coins for his childhood labors helped significantly to support him and his mother.

"Sometime during these years, his mother died. He couldn't remember her death. He thought he was about eight. He became a street urchin—delivering soup and performing odd jobs for whoever would give him a few coins. He became well-known around the brothels, but no one would tell him how she died. When I asked, he shrugged his shoulders and muttered, 'Infection?'

"His mother had a family, and they tried helping. Occasionally he would see them when he was especially desperate. His cousins and aunts were related to him, but he never knew how biological or filial the relationship was. In any case, he remembered a warm reception, a bath, food, and clothing. He would leave after a few days or a week, returning to the street life that was familiar and comfortable.

"The streets were always dangerous. He knew others of the same age who were killed because of some unexpected rage from those who managed the prostitutes, sold the drugs, or were dissatisfied with the sexual favors they were refused. Pho Bac became momentarily silent when talking about this, looking back into his own eyes for memories he quickly extinguished. Somehow, he always knew he might also be killed. He was clever, but he had scars to show his stealth did not always protect him completely. He, however, quickly interrupted by saying, 'But that's not the story.'

"When he was fourteen or fifteen, he learned that his being the son of a Vietnamese woman and an American officer could get him passage into to the United States. He applied to the US embassy in Vietnam, presented the counsel the shriveled piece of paper he kept all his life showing he was the son of an American, gained a sympathetic ear, and was sent to 'the country of golden streets' to live with a willing, sponsoring family in Saint Louis.

"Though he grew to love these people, he was not an easy charge. He skipped school, moved about with difficult kids, and was brought home in the arms of the police more than once. His behavior was always short of committing an outright crime, but his disturbances, more by association with others, became a matter of great concern. Despite the government's financial allotment, he and the family parted ways a mere two years later. He remembered them with affection but never felt they understood him.

"His adjustment was always difficult. It was difficult in Vietnam (where his light skin and blue eyes made him an American bastard and a pariah), and it was difficult in the United States (where his accent and cultural limitations always made him feel like a misfit).

"When he left Saint Louis, he came to New York, where he worked at a variety of jobs. Somehow, he passed the high school equivalency exam, got his social security card, and was able to find cheap lodging. He became involved with drug use. Because of bellicose behavior on the street one day, during a cocaine high, he was delivered to Bellevue Hospital.

"A young law student was on the same ward he was in—a beauty and another cocaine addict. These two were unlikely pairs, joined only by the circumstance of cocaine addiction. Pho Bac seemed a handsome man to me when I met him. His face had that peculiar blend of Asian and Occidental form so often apparent from mixed marriages. He was angular, thin, and because of his short-sleeved shirt, I noted a large tattoo in the shape of a dragon or mythic serpent along his right upper arm. His physique brought to mind a lithe runner in the marathon while his complexion was distinctly dark. I had no difficulty imagining his being attractive to a vulnerable woman on a drug-addiction ward. He described her to me as having deep-brown hair and as slightly tall in stature, with a puckered set of lips that completely charmed him. The chemistry was perfect, and the two became locked in a relationship. He was of the opinion that standing steadfastly beside her during the ups and downs of drug rehabilitation became a sealing ingredient that strengthened their connection.

"Their relationship continued upon discharge. Her drug problem was effectively kept a secret, and she returned to law school. She gave him a lead for a job at the law library—handling books, storage, and other odd jobs. Without telling her parents, she allowed him move into her apartment.

"The details that followed are not crucial to the story I'm telling you. We can only conjecture, as he jumped steps in the narrative to the subject of their marriage. She very much wanted to marry, but their finances were too slender for the match without her parents' help. The expected reaction from them followed. She was questioned about the reasonableness of her decision; a hundred reasons were given why the union should not be made legal, but she stood her ground. Her parents, liberals on the Chicago scene, capitulated, and they were married at a small Catholic church in Evanston.

"Pho Bac suffered greatly from his feeling of alienation as a Vietnamese. His memories remained there. Though he was able to love and be loved somewhat, he never felt complete—always having one mind in his home country filled with memories of suffering and turmoil and another in the United States. The girl's mother took it upon herself to research his background. Despite records of the war being available, his father could not be found. There was no trail of Lieutenant Colonel Stringe. Pho Bac said he often felt the wind was always in front of him, never at his back. He developed the idea that he should have his wedding repeated in Vietnam. He was able to prevail upon the family, and finally, the arrangements were made.

"When they arrived at the village, which he remembered to be his, it seemed as if relatives developed, grew, and populated his world in numbers he never imagined. The village wedding was large. After the ceremony, he was swept away by 'cousins' to a brothel. Awaking from severe inebriation the next day, he could not confidently tell his new wife he did not have sex with a prostitute. She was aghast. She wondered if this was some historical village hate that contrived such a postnuptial and, perhaps, was designed to rob her and Pho Bac of their happiness. More seriously, she feared he may have contracted AIDS or syphilis. She refused to have intercourse with him until he was thoroughly examined in the United States.

"Pho Bac put his hands on his head as he told me this part. I could see he was visibly upset with his sense of weakness at allowing himself to be used by the villagers claiming to be his family. He could not tell me for sure if these people really were connected to him.

"The next year was hell. The tests to assure his wife he was uninfected took six months to settle. He was not infected. His adjustment to marriage, her attending school all day, and his fundamental disquiet brought back his drug use. He connected with dealers and users again. Once, his wife came home and found the police rummaging through the apartment. She was appalled, and she feared the law school would find out and use this to keep her from graduating. A case was brought against Pho Bac. Since he was not caught while selling or in possession of drugs, but only severely implicated with his associated drug users, he was put on probation, which included forced rehabilitation. He was also threatened with divorce. His wife had long stopped using and was heavily invested in finishing law school. She told him if he didn't completely conform to the court's decision, she would leave him. His love for her was intense: his connection to everything that had any meaning to him, was his only mooring in a world of ambiguity and alienation. He began obeying every stricture of the decision. He religiously went to his rehab counselor and steered clear of all drug use.

"Nearly a year passed. Despite his good behavior, he felt adrift. He often thought of his mother and yearned for her. He wished he could connect to his father in some small way. He was neither an American nor a Vietnamese. He felt neither Caucasian nor Asian. His identity was in flux, a constantly changing stream. The villagers impressed him with the impossibility of any secure connection with the place where he was born. Whatever their memories, whatever they claimed, he felt unsecure with them. The names, places, and the orientations of familiar spaces that help us all feel secure or, at least, familiar with our world, were not there for him. All attempts to locate his real father failed. His only family was that of his wife, but he needed more. He needed a connection to Vietnam.

"The next unbelievable event happened just at this time. One day he was going home from his library job, and he was on one of the overhead trains in Chicago. There are millions of people with millions of railway stops and thousands of populated cars throughout the year, yet on this particular car—this particular day, at an unexpected hour or minute or second—he overheard Vietnamese being spoken. He lifted his head from the American magazine he was reading and noticed a middle-aged woman with a young man. They were talking rapidly in the friendliest manner. He paid attention and listened as he noted the mention of his village. He couldn't believe his ears. His years of loneliness, his feeling so adrift in the American world, and the pain of his losses all came together at that moment. More surprising was that the young man mentioned the name of someone Pho Bac had also thought of as a genuine relative was no longer alive. Astounded, he could forbear no longer; he called, across the train aisle, to the woman. He spoke in Vietnamese. He quickly told her he was from the village she mentioned and asked if she would mind talking to him for a moment. She said she would not mind, but her stop just arrived. He asked if he could get off with her and speak to her on the platform for just a little while. He promised not to bother further if nothing came of it. She agreed. She, the young man, and Pho Bac exited the car together.

"This Vietnamese woman was a biological relative of Pho Bac. She was his cousin. She knew him; she almost cried when she asked if he was Pho Bac. As the realization hit all of them, they could hardly control themselves. She was as moved as he was by the unlikelihood of their coming together on this train. She knew nothing of his wedding, since the now clearly false family (the villagers) never told her. She was living in Vietnam and was visiting her son, a student at the University of Chicago. She remembered his mother well; moreover, she remembered his visits to her house, his needing cleaning up and feeding, and his sudden disappearances.

She always wanted to find him and help him, but in the frenzy of the war days and its aftermath, digging him out of the detritus of the political miasma seemed impossible. She learned he had fled to the United States and never expected to see him again. It was a wonderful shock and surprise to hear his nickname again. Then they embraced, holding each other for a long time while her son looked on in amazement.

"That's the story.

"This was a luncheon moment with a surprise revelation by the usually taciturn Asian—an epiphany for me. You would think after sharing such a touching, personal tale with me, he might want to know who I was, where I was, and that sort of thing; but, no. He sat there staring at nothing in the direction of my face. I asked how he was now, and he said fine. He asked me, with a wan smile, what I thought of what he had told me. I said it was an amazing thing: meeting that woman on the train, restoring some connection to his past. I asked if he had seen her again. He told me many times. She comes often to see her son, and they always get together. Moreover, she telephones him from Vietnam. She is his only connection with his past. Others in her family have embraced him. He intends visiting there with his wife later this year. Then he told me he had to leave and thanked me for being an attentive listener. Of course, I thanked him for sharing his story with me. We shook hands and parted."

"Wow!"

"Yeah, wow! But you know, our soup never came."

"Waiter!"

MILLY'S CLASS

Milly had been in charge for well over fifteen years. The Juilliard School didn't know what to do with her. She began the adult program for pianists, and now it had blossomed into a fully-fledged evening division. She had aged but was still the doyen of teachers. The adults who stuck with her—playing their pieces to her focused and diligent ear and to each other over and over—could not disconnect. Why would they want to? This was one of those rare places that allowed you, for a hefty fee, to perform your heart out while knowledgeable listeners sat in total silence until you finished. Your bad notes, your poor rhythm, and your emotional limitations were all silently absorbed. Criticisms were kept a safe distance from reality. After the moment of music, you felt the week's preparation was well worth the effort—at least you got to find out what was truly unacceptable and what growth you had made. This was Milly's Repertoire Piano Class MV1241.

Every week, twice a week, the drama was played out. The cast was predictable. Sarah would come stumbling in late and then say she had to leave early.

"May I play first?"

She was fifty, a publisher of children's books, and she had frizzy blond hair, rarely combed. She had this distracted air: this wispy, willowy manner of never seeming to connect with others. Her nerdy style belied her piano skills. When she sat at one of the two seven-foot Steinways in the room, she played through the most difficult pieces by memory (some of which she had known all her life). Milly liked her because she could be depended upon. At a recital, she rarely had a memory lapse. Though the music that came from her seemed stilted and constrained, it was always complete. The average audience member would never detect the mechanical, uninspired nature of the notes. Her classmates complained about her only when she was absent.

"Sarah is always late. She walks in an hour after we begin. What's with her?"

She had her problems. Her husband developed Parkinsonism. This clearly took its toll on Sarah, making her seem more distracted and discombobulated. When speaking, she had this deceptive ebullience which expressed itself in a sing-song cheerful delivery. There was always something of the "crying clown" about her.

The rest of the class had a structured hierarchy. At the top of the pyramid, a little above Sarah, were the three piano giants: Bill, Oscar, and Taddeo. These three men dominated everyone in playing the piano and in directorial certainty. When they spoke, others were silent. Taddeo was the most vociferous, the alpha pianist.

"I think your rhythm is off," said Taddeo.

The subdued recipient of this jibe sat still as the silence persisted.

"Really? This is how Ashkenazi played it. I used his metronome markings."

Undeterred, Taddeo Suffner shrugged and said, "Have you ever listened to yourself? You should make a recording. I don't believe Ashkenazi would play like that. It's too slow. If you listen to yourself, you'll see what I mean."

His certainty was hypnotic and was as extensive as his extended abdomen. His corpulence was accentuated with his disheveled writer's garb. It beckoned a battle that no one wanted. The best classroom response was no response.

In this case, the victim simply mumbled, "Okay," and she returned to her seat.

Bill and Oscar did not strut like Taddeo. Their superiority to everyone was so clear, certified by Milly, that the two of them merely basked in the glory of their most praised performances. Bill was the neurosurgeon, a tight-lipped, but friendly, man who could memorize a Chopin ballade in a week. He was an erstwhile club jazz pianist, but he never hit a jazzy note in class. His success as a doctor and his dedication to his music avocation gave him such a lilt that he floated upon each session. It was rumored that he majored in music at Stanford but decided neurosurgery was a more sure thing. He often played concertos with Oscar, the two of them switching between accompaniment and solo. Oscar clearly respected Bill but played as well or better than Bill. His daytime job was computer programming at a major corporation. He dressed in the most casual attire—often plaid shirt and trousers, with extra pens in his breast pocket. He could be very stubborn, but he restrained from being the verbal bully Taddeo was.

Often, Oscar would take a position on something in the music which would ultimately lead him to say, "I don't care what you say. This is the way I see it. You can see it any way you like."

Since Oscar was acknowledged as the best musician, this often stopped the discussion cold. Yet he never went after someone the way Taddeo did.

After these giants of the amateur pianists, the field thinned out in terms of playing skills. Okeno was a good pianist, but he played like an obsessed Japanese, which, for the most part, she was.

She lived alone in a New York apartment. Her favorite people were cats (three of them), which she occasionally mooned over verbally, describing their antics. Once, she insisted on playing Scarlatti's *Cat's Fugue* during class sessions for six weeks! Every night she would hit the piano chromatic keys as the cat did in Scarlatti's head. She said she was trying to memorize the piece, and she dedicated each performance to one of her cats. Their names? Mumbo, Jumbo, and Beelzebub. Surely, she had Japanese equivalents, but these are the names we came to know. Okeno was tight-lipped otherwise. She was once irate because someone was following the playing on the music score.

"You are hurting the music. The pages are being turned too loudly!"

In fact, her voice drowned out the sound of both, but her imperial insistence brooked no opposition. The pages stopped turning, the other student at the piano began again with a languid and mealy smile, and Okeno was satisfied, if annoyed. When it came to Bach, she was quite impressive. Strangely, when it came to the Romantic composers, each piece sounded like Japanese Bach. Still, she was someone to admire, if you were down the talent ladder.

These were the stars. Why the four or five others were allowed in the class was somewhat of a mystery. Milly had her reasons. George could not come to the lower grade class because it was on a Monday night and his law partners never let anyone leave the office on a Monday before seven o'clock in the evening. Elsa became a student because the other class for the fourth level was full. Mario had been coming for fifteen years, never memorized anything, but struggled. Others had suggested to Milly that he didn't belong, but she had affection for him. Occasionally, he played rather well, though never from memory.

Milly would say, "There are some good things...some good things? Have you ever looked at the inventions? They might help you. You are so musical."

She had repeatedly tried having him take the lower classes. He did comply, but those students were so behind him that he couldn't stand hearing them. He was in purgatory: not good enough for the stars and too good for the planets. There was an ongoing agitation between Milly caring for him and her frustration that he couldn't play well enough. Once, Taddeo blatantly asked Milly to push Mario down a notch. This got to Mario, and he was livid. In his mind, what bothered him wasn't that he thought he was so good; it was that he was struggling to reach the alpha summit, and he could not accept a demotion. He loved the piano, though he knew his love was irrational. He knew he could improve to acceptable limits and hoped for it. Being demoted in the process was simply too much to bear. He certainly practiced enough. Each day he would go through the Bach preludes and fugues. He played them way below tempo at first. It took years just to approach their being musical. Poor Mario. He was a struggling nonprofessional musician and the only class member who didn't have any background of music school. He began his piano playing as an adult. His ambition was to play well enough for a chamber music trio. Meanwhile, he was barely tolerated by the uppers in the night class.

Between Mario and the alphas was Lorelei. Lorelei was in her early seventies, had known Milly for more years than anyone else, and was a capable pianist. She had a delicate touch, and occasionally, her playing rose to heights challenged only by the alphas. She was becoming blind from macular degeneration, and she could no longer read music from the required distance of two feet or more. She hunched over the piano because of severe arthritis. She memorized all her old pieces. The class absorbed the fact that she might repeat them over and over. She had a two-bedroom apartment in Manhattan, and Milly often stayed with her. Milled lived in Stony Brook, Long Island, and she found two days of classes at Juilliard too much for commuting. Clearly, the two women liked each other, but a strange formality remained between them. Lorelei was psychologically astute. She seemed to see beneath the posturing of the alphas and often smiled when their excesses became obvious. Accepting her relative blindness, her arthritic back, and her living alone seemed part of her character. Everyone uttered her name, Lorelei, with a sweet lyrical song tone revealing the affection they felt for her unassuming excellence with all its flaws.

Milly was the glue that held this mélange together. She was the first to suggest to the school to develop an evening division. Now, other teachers competed with her for students. She chafed whenever one of hers went over to another. Once, though, she suggested to Mario that he go to Mr. Tschkovitz. Mr. Tschkovitz would have none of Mario's ilk. He sent him an email saying he feared Mario would hamper other students' development. Milly was stuck with Mario.

Milly had her rivals. Felicia seemed jealous. She and Milly shared piano classrooms. In the early days of the program, Felicia had her five o'clock evening class before Milly's at seven o'clock. Felicia would put the lights out, put the piano seat at the other end of the room, or turn the AC way down. Milly would fume quietly and simply carry on. Once, Felicia began a semester with a new Concerto class, and this attracted the piano alphas. Milly, for the first time, made a comment expressing that she expected loyalty. She also began allowing concerto playing in her solo class. This seemed to stem the outflow of her top students.

Milly was Austrian, but she grew up in Paris. She was a promising soloist, with a career she abbreviated for marriage. The Conservatoire de Paris—home of Franck, Debussy, Delibes, and Poulenc—was her home, and she often brought up her pedigree.

"At the Academy, we had to learn Bach fugues in all their parts: memorized, first soprano, then alto, then tenor, then bass. Each voice had to be learned independently. I did not like doing this, but it was very good to do. You may try it, even though learning five-part fugues was not easy."

She spoke in a charming French accent, melodic but firm. Whether she pursued her concert career or not, she was a very serious musician, and her attitude affected everyone. Amazingly, she would sit from half past five to half past seven and listen to varying levels of playing music. Her comments were at the end of each person's piece.

"Does anyone have anything to say about Mario's nocturne?"

She would wait for a response. If Mario played poorly or the class thought he played poorly, there would be silence. The silence was a condemnation.

Then she would say, "There were many good things. Did you take harmony? I didn't hear the key changes."

She would lean forward and make a disappointed facial mask, announcing, "You know, when you play mezzo forte, it sounds like double forte. Were you nervous?"

Of course, everyone was nervous in the class. Many excuses for dubious performances hinged on the comment, "I was nervous." Even Taddeo used it. So did Bill and Oscar.

Milly's goal was to keep her class going and keep her students. Felicia's concerto class threatened hers but so did drop-outs. As a serious musician who fully believed in the catechism that every piano performance was a bow to the music gods, she was as polite as she could be. She once asked another student, Roman, to try going to the lower class because there had been complaints that he didn't belong at the level of Bill, Oscar, and Taddeo. Roman was crushed, and he left altogether, but Milly believed keeping her alpha players was more of a sacred duty than not responding to their aggravations with poorer players.

If an ignorant visitor came to the class, she would see none of the tension extant. Everyone was polite, quiet, and raptly paid attention to others' playing. Milly would seem useless and oblivious, mouthing niceties that were clearly unhelpful. Nothing could be further from the truth from this idle observation. There was a subsurface turbulence of pre-storm-like proportions. Waves of frustration and anger boiled beyond view. Milly heard every note, and every utterance was designed to criticize and teach. This was the extreme reverse of a tranquil moment in learning the piano. The serene Milly kept violence in check. The class without her would have been a wolf pack tearing apart the carcass of music for the award of the best bite. The lesser predators would skulk away, sulking at their failures of the evening and hoping to improve enough to be blessed by Milly's deific, but terrifying, smile. Each student, good or bad, had practiced hours the preceding week. This momentary performance was all they had to show for it. Nerves, memory lapses, and musical snafus marred their output, and Milly was gently, but firmly, unforgiving.

She would say, "You must respect the composer. You must honor his creation."

Everyone knew when they failed. No grades were needed. Everyone knew their rank, and everyone fought within themselves to improve it. Rationalizations that it was merely an adult recreation that cost a lot of money were not truly believed. Whether it was genetics or limitations of talent, each had to live within their self-realization that the truth of who they were was there in the musical performance. There was no escape from this truth. There was no escape from Milly. She may have looked like a meager four-feet-eleven redhead, but her musical power was hidden in her small frame.

Year after year, this continued. Oscar and Bill won piano competitions. Taddeo made a CD, which he handed out pridefully to the class. Okeno mastered the Bach *Italian Concerto* and played it from memory at the correct tempo; this was no small accomplishment. New people came and went, defeated by the ferocity of the unspoken battle. Mario improved, but he could not bring himself to memorize his pieces, a requirement needed to fully please Milly and silence the alphas. Lorelei's vision got worse. She sometimes needed to be told who was sitting next to her. She had back surgery. Always there, however, was the music. The class changed. Everyone seemed older, more certain. There was almost no humor. Any joke made fell flat.

The consensus was the class was made of addicts (music addicts). The nucleus accumbens is the region of the brain that responds to dopamine stimulation brought to bear by cocaine. This same organ was believed to be stimulated by music. Constant practicing reinforced the responsivity of the brain. The students were hooked. Unless they got their quotient of music input every day, each week, they were unable to feel comfortable. No music led to addiction withdrawal. Milly created an ashram of addicts.

Even when the school year was over, the class met at Gerald's apartment, a few blocks from the school. He would offer cheese, wine (which no one dared drink until after they played), and vegetable dip. He was a long-standing near alpha member of the class who once approached Mario to ask him whether Milly didn't like him. He felt she was too critical and she never seemed to praise his playing. After he won a major amateur piano competition in Moscow, he felt he could relax. He was accepted into the alphas and enjoyed, at least, the belief that Milly thought he was adequate. His own humility made him have little interest in displaying the arrogant alpha characteristics of the top players. He was comfortable within himself and generously offered his nearby apartment for the after-school recitals. The addicts had to get their fix any way they could. School or no school, they had to be heard.

Then Milly began showing her age even more. The school frustrated her. The school told her part-time teachers did not need an office. She was moved to limbo. She no longer had a room with a piano in it to practice, the essential ingredient of a faculty member of the austere school. She only had to show up to teach her classes. The aura of professorship had been removed, and she felt the denigration. She began cutting classes short, buying tickets instead to prominent recitals at Avery Fisher Hall or Carnegie Hall. Once, she made a dinner engagement with friends, having the school call to say the class was suspended for the night. She began to forget the origin of pieces, and she got confused as to holiday dates. For a long while, this was overlooked. She seemed to come back to herself, and all was well again.

One day she just didn't show up. Leadership was gone. The alphas played their pieces, and others listened. The underlings were afraid to play among the predators. They began to leave early. Where was Milly? The world seemed to be devolving. The force of gravity disappeared. The center did not hold. Where was she? It was night, so the evening division office was closed. There was no way to find out what happened to her. Lorelei said she hadn't come to stay with her. When she telephoned Milly's home number, only her recorded message answered. The class became a blinded whale, floating but confused and distraught.

The highly organized, ritualized, standardized, and required organization came to a halt. The fear in each remaining student's mind was about the uncertainty of the long-held certainty. On a Thursday night, there was Millie's piano class. The week was designed to meet this internally desired operation. Without Milly, the entire meaning of life was held in suspension. They could transfer to another class, but it would not have Milly. Her essence was the quintessence of their desire, their weekly experience. They were not wandering and aimless zombies, but the feeling just approached such a nightmare.

Milly was ill. She had a small stroke. Her hypertension was not well-controlled. She didn't take her medication the way she was supposed to. The depression that plagued her when her husband was hit by a car twelve years ago re-emerged. She would not be teaching for at least six months. A refund was offered but most transferred to another teacher just for the semester. Everyone wondered how she would be after the recuperation, but, mostly, everyone wanted the class back.

Six months later, just after a snow storm, Milly returned. She was more inward and subdued, but alert. She sat in her usual chair with everyone asking her about her health. A half hour of well wishes and light talk took up the first session. People were spent. Silence came.

Milly spoke, "Okay. Who will play first? Oscar, you go."

Oscar played, and the class went on as if in a normal fashion. Everyone knew Milly was deteriorating, but her presence was all that was required. Taddeo insisted on doing Beethoven's *Op. 111*. After he had finished, he asked if he could do it again.

"That's enough!" Milly said in an uncharacteristic show of irritation. "Others have to play."

Her voice was soft. She wouldn't alienate Taddeo. He elected to overlook her abrasive tone and got up from the piano.

"Mario, are you going to play?" Milly asked.

Mario had started working on the Beethoven's *Piano Sonata No. 2* in A major. This was not one of Beethoven's more difficult sonatas, but the last movement was challenging (with its arpeggios running up and down the keys). Mario's idea was to use it as a learning piece. He decided to play the last two movements. Others had often used the class for tryouts, but those were the alphas. Mario was being a little daring by holding others to listen over a twenty-minute period. Still, he thought to himself, If others can make me listen to a forty-minute piece, why can't I do twenty?"

Mario played. He finished, and there was dead silence in the room. Milly looked glum. The negative response was like a thick material that could be cut with a dull knife. The absence of words dominated as a scream.

"How long have you been working on this?" Milly asked.

Mario was puzzled. He said before he played that he had been working on it for a couple of weeks, and he wanted to try it out. Here she was asking a question about what she had already heard.

"A couple of weeks, like I said."

Milly was on the assault.

"Did you practice the A major arpeggios? It sounds like you don't know what an arpeggio is."

Mario was taken aback. Milly rarely attacked, but this was an attack.

"Yes, I practiced the arpeggios. They are difficult in this piece. I think I can have them by next week."

Milly looked around sullenly and then said, "Anyone else wants to say anything?"

Taddeo mumbled, "It is what it is."

Mario shot back, "What do you mean, 'It is what it is'?"

The silence became a condemning gloom.

"Okay. Who's next?" Milly asked and brought everyone back.

That week, Milly made a phone call to Mario. This was not unusual. She called from time to time to compliment, encourage, and ask about practice issues. She lived alone with her two dogs since her husband's death. The class was her world.

"Mario, how do you think you did Thursday night?"

"Well, I was struggling to get those A major arpeggios in line. I think I can do it in another week or so."

"Why don't you play the Beethoven in the five o'clock class and just listen to the seven o'clock repertoire class? Or you could play just the third movement. That went well."

"Sure, I could do that."

"Good. I'll see you Thursday. Keep practicing."

"I always practice."

The following Thursday, after the phone call, Mario showed up at the time agreed upon to play the last movement of the Beethoven. He had worked on it diligently, and he was looking forward to how it would play. He was also prepared for the third movement in the repertoire class. There were three other students in the classroom, all familiar to Mario.

Milly looked at him, as if he was entirely unexpected, pulled herself into an erect position and said, "Do you want to play something?"

Mario was flummoxed. He recalled the phone call and the plan laid out by Milly and could not believe the question.

"Well, you remember the phone call, don't you? I was supposed to play the last movement of the Beethoven in this class and the second movement in the repertoire class?"

"You are no longer in the repertoire class. I called the school and had you transferred to this class. You will get a refund from the school."

Mario couldn't believe what he was hearing. The aggression shown by this behavior was so far beyond anything he had seen in the fifteen years with Milly. He paused and looked at her.

"Are you for real?" he uncharacteristically said.

He had always respected Milly and would never before have spoken to her in this way. Her behavior was triggering a wave of anger he didn't know he had toward her.

"Do you remember what you said on the phone?" Mario asked.

She looked perplexed. She did not remember the phone conversation.

"How could you go to the school and do such a thing?" After a pause, he continued, "You know, it's a class. It's not a judged recital. We're supposed to be learning. Suddenly, the learning class turned into a finished performance. This was never the way it was supposed to be."

"Do you know what happened when you left the class last week? Taddeo and Oscar became excited and said they didn't want you in the class anymore. You were not at the level of this class. Even Bill, who never talks about others, stayed quiet. He leaned on the desk right there." She pointed to the only desk in the room. "They were angry with your Beethoven. Did you practice your arpeggios?"

Mario was so frozen by these revelations; he was speechless. On the one hand, he had underestimated the hostility these people felt for him. He thought about how Marsha, another student, played much worse than he, was never prepared, but never elicited the reaction he was getting. He began questioning what he had done to engender such behavior. Certainly, he should not have played such a long piece, nearly twenty minutes, but Taddeo had done this many times, uncaring about the burden on his listeners.

More puzzling was Milly's complete lack of professionalism and the way she was threatened by these three men. He quickly reasoned that she felt intimidated and worried that they would leave the class if he stayed. Her fear sent her to the school administration office to arrange the transfer. Her rising dementia had to be playing a part in all those decisions. She really couldn't clearly think about the situation. Mario could not imagine over the past fifteen years that she would act in such a bold and unreasonable fashion. He considered that the long-standing regular music class was likely ending. If Milly could not handle the matters with more decorum, the class was losing its meaning anyway. What student would want to play and participate in a music program with a teacher who wouldn't remember from week to week what had happened?

Mario planned to leave the program. Over the following weeks, he stopped going to class. He received a call from the school administrator—a lovely sounding woman named Phyllis, who was surprisingly sympathetic to him. She admitted she had noticed diminishing memory and astuteness in Milly. Other than this, she could not explain the unexpected way Milly had attacked him. In any case, the school was willing to reimburse half his tuition. Mario thought that was generous but was reluctant to take it. In the end, he took the payback and left the school.

The succeeding weeks gave Mario plenty of time to reflect on what had happened. He was not sure how bad his playing was and how much of a factor this was in the class ejecting him.

He recalled many compliments over the years. He missed the intellectual discussions about music and realized he would lose the wisdom of the unhappy superior players. Their sullen seriousness always perplexed him. There was rarely humor in the class. Any attempt he made to lighten the atmosphere was met with a silent lack of response. He noted that this episode, which he saw as extreme and unwarranted, happened at a time when the alpha players were gaining recognition in amateur circles for playing concertos and solo concerts. Perhaps, even though he had improved over the years, his presence made them uncomfortable. After all, who wants to be associated with someone who cannot play as well as they can? Yet their tolerance of Marsha has remained a mystery.

He was most bothered by the now-established fact that Milly was willing to destroy a long-standing friendly relationship with so little concern. He hoped her dementia was not severe and that she would be able to manage her lonely widowhood. He did not wish her ill. There were no winners in this story.

Mario lingered over his thoughts, obsessively returning to unanswerable questions: What had he done to deserve such opprobrium? Had he been surly or disrespectful? Could this degree of frustration have been engendered only by his bad playing? Was he really that bad? What crowd mentality caused the upswell of contempt and an insistence that he leave?

He was never to know the truth.

"Hello!"

It was two years later, and Lorelei and Mario bumped into each other at the philharmonic. Mario spoke first, as Lorelei hadn't seen him.

"Remember me? Mario?"

"How are you, Mario? Nice to see you." Her mellifluous voice of genuine welcoming always worked to soothe him. "Are you still playing?"

"I practice every day, but I've been blackballed from Juilliard. They won't let me into any piano class."

"Really? That doesn't sound right. Did you audition?"

"Yes, three times. My big mistake was disagreeing with my placement in Piano II. I think my protestation was the end of me. Now they keep saying things like 'Unfortunately, all our places are filled this term.'"

Lorelei stood in the street with her philharmonic program in her hand, not sure what to say.

"Why won't they let you in? You were a student for so long. I don't understand." She was genuinely troubled by Mario's announcement.

"I think the new management sees me as a kind of troublemaker, someone that might disrupt their classes. The stormy departure of Milly left a bad taste in their mouths, and my objecting to my first placement simply confirmed their concerns. Also, Phyllis, the new director of the evening division seemed overwhelmed with my protestations after their three rejections. She refused to meet with me to resolve anything. She became mean-spirited and stopped talking to me, and now there is no redress. I wrote a letter to the president of the school and he never answered."

"Oh my. I'm so sorry, Mario. I hope you stay with the piano. You really were getting better."

"Thank you, Lorelei. Have you seen Milly? How is she?"

"No. She disappeared. I don't know anything about her. She doesn't stay with me anymore. I think she's still on Long Island, but I really don't know."

"Well. I guess that's it."

"Nice seeing you, Mario."

"Thanks, Lorelei. You too."

THE STORY OF Z

I t was the time before the movie *Z* was made, but it was in the same precinct, the same neighborhood, that those reported events took place. It was——, the town in Thessaloniki where Hardeki was killed by the policeman. My Greek barber, Billy, was a twelve-year-old boy then. He was beaten by his father every day. Just three days before his father—who was near death—died, Billy asked his father, over the telephone, why he beat him every day.

"You were a bad boy. You needed it," his father answered.

"Why every day?" Billy asked. "Wasn't there a day when I was not bad?"

His father never answered. They hung up. His father died.

Billy was fearful. He was a good boy, but he never felt comfortable. He befriended a dog and called him "Hardeki."

"It wasn't really a dog," he explained. "It was a mutt: part regular dog, part wolf."

He would often hug him—feeling the comfort and security of the animal, knowing in his heart the Hardeki would not let anyone hurt him. If anyone came near Billy, the dog would growl protectively. Billy would have to hold him back.

The Z Party ("Z means 'life,'" Billy was careful to explain) was holding elections. In the movie with the same name as the political party, Yves Montand is coming to host a rally, but the conservative, incumbent opposition party means to break up the meeting. They have trouble getting a hall and trouble printing announcements. There is general knowledge that Yves's character, the character putting himself up for election, may be attacked. The decision is to have the rally anyway. You come to admire Yves, his courage, his determination, his feeling that nuclear war must be prevented. You feel his position is more than that of empty political opportunism. There is a suggestion that the United States may be behind some of the incumbent party's determination to eliminate Yves. There is a great deal of movement. A great deal of energy. The movie engages you till you're wondering how it is all going to end. It's hard not to take sides. Costa-Gavras, the director, wants to tell the story of injustice, political dirt, and human tragedy. He refers to a real tale, and you are made to feel that reality as the story unfolds.

It is a real story, and Billy was there. He was aware of the rally, and he had personal contact with the policeman who murdered Lambrakis, the real-life person that Montand's character portrays. He met this policeman whose name was known to be——("I can't tell you this," Billy says; "he is alive in my hometown. I can't tell you."). He knew him before he became an officer, before the stars were planted on his lapels.

"He was a son of a bitch. He was so powerful he scared the hell out of me. He didn't wear a uniform. He was a good-looking big man; you couldn't miss him when he walked down the street. No uniform, but you knew he was a policeman. Some kind of secret police. You knew to be afraid."

Billy's dog was not a full wolf, but he had enough wolf in him to excite a fearful twelve-year-old.

Whenever Billy felt threatened, he would cry out in a rage that Hardeki understood well. "Go! Haardehhkeee!"

And the wolf/dog would lunge at the person who was frightening Billy. The dog and the boy depended on and loved each other.

The policeman would often come to Billy's section of town to demonstrate power, collect money, and push people around.

He would notice Billy and his dog and ask in nonsensical prose, "What is that dog?"

What is a boy to answer when asked such a question?

"Nothing," Billy answered.

"That dog shouldn't be here!"

Silence. Finally, the policeman would leave. He would walk out onto the street and yell at someone to move something, or call to another person to bring him something. He always spoke in a harsh commanding voice. No one would disobey. Billy hated him.

As the bond between Billy and his dog grew, Billy's father found it more difficult to beat him. The dog would growl and threaten. His father was afraid of the dog. One day, the dog attacked Billy's father. The dog had to be pulled away. His father's pants were torn, but the skin was not touched. Billy's father was enraged.

The next day, Billy saw the policeman. He was putting poison around, but Billy didn't know this. He saw him place something near the house, on the street, but he didn't connect this with anything. He was a twelve year old. Suspicion was not part of his armament. Shortly after, Hardeki died (obviously poisoned). Billy was crushed. For weeks, he felt miserable, alone, at a loss, but there was no one to tell. He could only engrain the experience in his mind, remember it with passion, and perhaps, tell it to a customer in his barber shop someday.

The same policeman killed Yves Montand's character in the movie, and, in real life, killed Lambrakis. He was promoted, and he began wearing a uniform, with stars on the uniform's lapel. Many wondered if the stars were only for the murder.

Greece changed politics and trials were finally held; the policeman was convicted for the murder of Lambrakis. He was placed in jail for twenty years. After shooting the movie, the character playing the policeman left the set and had a cigarette.

I once asked Billy if he knew of the movie "Z."

He said, "I'm going to tell you a story that no other Greek knows."

He became excited and told me the tale of Hardeki and his father.

As I paid my bill for my haircut, I could see that Billy was near tears. He was remembering his dog/wolf, his father, the policeman, and the movie, and he could not bear the feelings it created. I suddenly saw he had drooping rings under his eyes, and the eyes expressed a tragedy in his being I had never seen before. I paid my bill and opened the door to leave.

"Billy," I said, "I know your father was wrong."

I left him standing there looking forlorn in my direction as I turned my back to enter the street.

PELICANO

Almost every day is beautiful in Puerto Vallarta. Horizontal clouds spread across Banderas Bay, dividing the azure sky from the sea's surface, the edge of which can be seen in the far distance. Helados Jiminez watched the clouds become translucent wisps that fan out as the mild east winds blew them in his direction. He dreamily watched the changing white forms as he sat on a cast iron–painted bench near the beach, at the water's edge. His gaze moved from the delicate symphony of the quiet sky toward the crescent-shaped Mexican shore and then drifted casually toward the more exciting plummeting pelicans before him.

These large gray-white birds, so awkward and unsculptured at rest, intrigued Helados only slightly as he watched them in their effortless flight. In their groundless medium, their proportions were perfect. Wings and beak aligned, they sailed forty, maybe fifty feet, above the sea waves—moving back and forth along the beach-line, studying the water for food. Suddenly, one of them altered its course, almost stopping midair. Its entire body moved from the horizontal position to the vertical. Its beak pointed downward, and its wings swept back; the avian marvel would plummet into the shallow Pacific waters to engulf the fish dinner it had spied. For the tourist, this was a spectacular scenario, but for Helados, it was merely an ever-present pastime—something to help lull him into the hypnotic peace that spliced together the hours between work and more work.

Helados was a poor, but not unhappy, man. He worked for Sandro, the mustached, muscular owner of one of the three scuba diving concessions in the village. It was a tourist business. Every morning at eight, the two men met where the public beach stopped: the private beach of the Golden Mano Hotel. Helados would haul the oxygen tanks, halters, masks, beer and ice, ropes, and a large plastic gasoline jar out of the jeep and into Sandro's boat. He and Sandro worked like brothers. They had known each other all of their lives. Sandro, however, was ambitious, and he planned a future for himself in a way Helados could not begin to conceive. Helados had a simple view of life. He expected nothing. He believed in his *Jesus Cristo*, and his wife and child. His work was a labor of necessity, and he demanded it should satisfy nothing else within him. The pay Sandro gave Helados was managed carefully. A tourist might spend over 3,000 pesos on a beer, but Helados could enjoy one for a mere 1,000. Besides, his wife was given almost every peso to manage as she deemed wise. There was no envy in him as he helped prepare Sandro's business for the day. Sandro appreciated his old friend's philosophy. He paid him well for his loyalty. It was more than a business arrangement.

Helados and Margarita lived in a small house left to them by his father-in-law, a man who loved his only daughter and saved from his shoe-shine business to secure her a permanent roof over her head. In return, his daughter loved his memory and her house with religious intensity. She felt it possessed the spirit of her youth. In its walls, she recognized not only her memories but also the loving personalities of her parents. It was only a year after her marriage to Helados that her father and mother had died. It was a freakish accident, the kind that the priest quietly alludes to the strange and unexpected ways of the Lord. Her parents were walking along the narrow and winding mountain road, north of the village, when a man from their own town driving foolishly, trying to get past a Volkswagen around the curve. The truck would have missed Margarita's parents if their one-time friend had given a mere six inches as leeway. But he underestimated his clearance. He should never have tried overtaking anyway. He knew that many accidents had occurred along the same road. The driver was forced to abandoned his friends and his village. He was ruined. His old friends and neighbors were intolerant, unable to accept the idea that he should have killed two of them. If he had hit tourists, he would not have felt the pressure to leave. There was no trial. The only compensation for Helado's wife was the house she worshiped as if it were part of herself.

Margarita and Helados loved each other. She often laughed at his name, but if she tried calling him Hector, he would scowl at her. He enjoyed his nickname. As a boy, he was known for his love of ice cream. Whether he had a few pennies or he was just asked what he wanted by his uncle, the answer was always the same: *helado*. He was a marvel to others because he always remained skinny despite his enormous consumption of ice cream. As he grew older, his interest in beer never matched that of his adolescent cronies. While they had *Dos Equis* or Corona, he had <u>helado</u>. And now, as he sat between the morning equipment delivery and the afternoon pickup, staring at the pelicans diving for fish, he ate the ice cream bar he purchased for half the tourist price from the white helado cart cruising the beachfront.

Helados was not a completely ignorant man. His family saw to it that he received the required Catholic education. It was limited in its scope, but he could read (and even understand) some of the Latin words at Sunday Mass. He felt disappointment when the reforms came and the Mass was performed in Spanish. This education, as it was, did nothing to allay his natural superstitious beliefs. When he was young, he spent many days at the home of Senora Juarez, the woman known to be a descendant of one of the Aztec tribes that had settled in Guadalajara. She was said to know witchcraft, but Helados never saw any. All he experienced were her many stories of revenge, sacrifice, and magical portents. She never told where these stories came from. They always happened to someone who knew the person who told her the story. This didn't matter. Helados was an avid listener and the direct opposite of a skeptic. He believed what he was told. He believed unswervingly in magic.

These two polarities of his mental existence—Catholicism and magic—juxtaposed against his loyalty and honesty toward his friends and family and constituted the substance of his character. He never showed these qualities outwardly; they were merely part of his style. He rarely went to church. But he was glad Margarita went to mass every day. He was sure the benefits of her devotion would be passed onto him. He hoped this would include protection against the potential punishment for his one indiscretion—Lucinta.

Helados was loyal, but he had his appetites. This was the way he rationalized his bed adventures with Lucinta. It may seem peculiar to more sophisticated minds that he would be able to occasion-ally enjoy the pleasures of Lucinta's thighs and, simultaneously, see no sin of marital corruption against Margarita. But that was the honest truth. Margarita was his wife. She had to understand Lucinta was merely another woman. In fact, Margarita knew about the affair and saw it as a necessary part of her marital happiness. She knew Lucinta to be a clean woman; she knew that Lucinta, as a widow, needed someone occasionally; and she saw Lucinta as a friend, though the two never talked about their shared lover (that would have been unspeakable). The threesome maintained this "secret" relationship for many years—at least six. In spite of this,

Helados sustained a considerable foreboding if Margarita should ever find out about his sinful indiscretion. He deeply felt he was wrong. He often wondered whether he would receive a punishment for this transgression against the laws of the Church. Though he would never suspect Margarita of witchcraft, he certainly knew of other men's wives putting spells on their husbands for infidelity. After each daytime visit to Lucinta's, he would inspect Margarita's face for signs of anger, but he never saw any. He assumed that the church, Padre Oscar, and Christ were watching over him. His mood was made sanguine by these mental reassurances. As he went to work every day, he would stop before the door of the Church of Guadalupe and stare up at the huge crown of the Virgin topping the front tower. He would then imagine the altar of the Virgin and genuflect, saying a blessing and asking for her continued protection. He would then say "Hail Mary" many times, thanking her for another day of peace.

Between delivery and pickup, there was nothing to do. The boat was out with its usual six to ten tourists hiding under the stretched canopy to avoid the hot sun, until they could don the gear delivered by Helados and dive into the exotic Pacific coral world beneath the sea surface.   The jeep was parked to the side. The police would never consider giving it any trouble. Sometimes Margarita would come and sit with him on the bench, but today she was home. She was enjoying the lassitude of her second nascent pregnancy by languishing into a long siesta, with her son lying by her side.

Helados sat alone watching the pelicans and the tourists. He saw boys with iguanas accosting well-dressed Yankees. He prided himself on his ability to identify where tourists came from. These were Yankees, there was no doubt. Most tourists were, anyway. The boys asked in English if the lady would want a picture of the animal. Helados laughed. The boy was only seven or eight years old, but he spoke like a huckster of fifty years.

"Two dollars?" The lady smiled. "That's too much."

The boy knew he had a possible sale.

"I'll give you a dollar," the lady said.

Helados was shocked when he heard the boy answer, "Too cheap. Too cheap. Ten dollars."

The man chimed in, "We'll give you one dollar. Take it or leave it."

The boy nodded, and they began taking pictures. As soon as they had taken a few shots of the animal from various angles, the boy became angry. He grabbed the iguana and told them they owed him ten dollars. Helados understood that José, (that was his name) expected only one picture to be taken for the single dollar. José counted ten pictures taken and wanted that amount of money. The couple walked away after offering two dollars to quiet him. The woman's smile had disappeared. Both were feeling the culture and language barrier. The man threatened to get a policeman if the boy did not take the reasonable amount of money offered. José came to Helados for help.

"These *Americanos* are cheap. They owe me ten dollars," said José.

"Do you want to sell the iguana?" Helados asked with a chuckle. "You know the animal itself is not worth that much. Why don't you take the money the *turistas* are offering you, and stop making trouble for yourself? If the police come, you will get nothing."

Feeling abandoned by one of his own kind, José took the money offered and cursed the unknowing couple in Spanish. This only made Helados laugh. The boy ran down the street with his iguana resting on his shoulder as if it were a tree stump, its strange prehistoric head staring passively at nothing of meaning while its long, narrow tail dragged behind. The couple laughed, and Helados laughed even harder.

It was a lazy day in February. There were many tourists experiencing the constant sunny 76 degrees that Helados took for granted. He enjoyed watching them with their variety of T-shirts and hats. Their pale white skins intrigued him when he judged the color against his own ocher-brown. Many of them carried large bags containing silver jewelry bought from his friends at 200 percent markups. He enjoyed this world of two worlds. It was always good for a laugh. Soon the boat would be back, emptied of its hotel guests. He would have to transfer the equipment again to the jeep and take them into storage until tomorrow. The bright sunshine soothed him. The pelicans were diving. His eye caught the movement of one particular bird as it made the plunge.

At this moment of time, Helados's life changed. He knew something was peculiar to the dive of this pelican. He watched its descent with that cocked head of wonder as one sees in a small animal when it perceives a sound it cannot localize or comprehend. The large avian hunter came plummeting out of its serenity, poised to consume another victim of its ineluctable passion for survival (streamlined to what its part of the evolutionary niche had provided). The ordinary, the expected, was not to be. Instead, the bird demolished itself by insensibly smashing its body into the thick grainy sands of the Vallarta beach.

How this refined flying creature from nature had managed to miss its intended prey in the sea and pummel itself onto the beach instead was of absolutely no concern to Helados. He heard the cry of the crowd that had chanced to witness what he had just seen. He canceled this perception, deciding at once that the experience was unique to himself. He was alone. His mind took him over. There was no world of fellow experiencers; there was only himself. He himself was stunned with himself. He had experienced a unique self-nature intertwine. He had experienced magic. His mind painted his own picture: the great black pelican had been possessed by the nature god, a subsidiary of the Great God, and because the bird had transgressed, he was condemned to be deceived by himself. There was no escape except by appeasement.

Appeasement. Helados heart had been entered. He had seen the darkened, shadowed, flying miracle. He was possessed.

He sat. He stood. He sat. He was not sure what to do. People gathered around the bird talking busily about their amazement. No one spoke of sensing it was an omen, but Helados could think of nothing else. He could not comprehend its meaning to him then, but he knew there was a meaning. For certain, there was future dread, something bad was to happen. These thoughts pushed all others out of his mind. He saw someone carry the dead bird away. He ran home to tell his beautiful, comforting, dark-haired Margarita.

At first Margarita almost convinced him there was nothing to fear. As she promised, she went to church that very night the bird had fallen from the sky. When Padre Oscar said the mass, she grasped her rosary beads tightly and prayed for Helados. When she received communion, she swallowed the wafer thinking of him. As she left the church with her friends, she saw her husband waiting sheepishly at the street corner. He grasped her two hands as she approached and asked her if all went well. She still wore her mother's lace shawl on her head, and she looked like the Virgin herself. Even with his anxiety, Helados was touched by her tenderness and love. He became quieted.

The dark avian occurrence and Helados's feeling of dread, however, became meshed. It was, indeed, as if he had been cursed.

"What have you done to deserve this?" Margarita asked when he announced his condition to her.

He became silent. What have I done? he asked himself. There is only Lucinta. His thoughts drifted away into misery.

Finally, she convinced him to see Padre Oscar with her. As much as he believed he had merged with an omen was how much he wanted to believe in the power of the padre. He went to see the priest with great hope. Padre Oscar spoke kindly to him. The educated man thought soothing reassurances would help. He told

Helados of Saint Francis—how the great man loved birds and how his love of birds and their freedom was a part of his message of love to mankind.

"The unfortunate pelican was ill. God's creatures must all pass into another life. It was merely the bird's time. Why turn this unfortunate matter into a frightening belief. God would not want this. Be at peace."

The padre felt he was eloquent, yet down to earth. He felt Helados would be mollified by this explanation. In addition, the padre went on to ask if there was any special problem in Helados's life that required a confession. Had there been any sin troubling him and that might be causing him to make too much of this experience with the bird? Helados was actually considering an answer to the last question when the padre interrupted him by taking a cross from his desk drawer. If the good priest had waited just another moment, he might have solved the problem and would have prevented a great deal of misery. But what is apparent to the observer is often missed by the participant. The father told Helados that the cross was supposedly kissed by Saint Teresa of Ávila, a Spanish woman who actually spoke to Christ, and it had great powers. He was lending this to Helados. It was too precious to give. The loan was a testimony of his faith in Margarita's husband. When peace returned to him, Helados could return it.

"Pray with it daily," the priest cautioned, "and this pain in your soul will be resolved."

He also insisted he should attend mass for a week. They parted with smiles and clasping hands.

Helados obeyed completely. He did not even feel strange being at mass every day with the women and the old men. Each day as he returned from helping Sandro, he kissed the blessed cross of Saint Teresa. He prayed on this magical power and began to feel some comfort again.

Some dared to speculate later whether it was God's weakness or Evil's strength that led to the following events. There were those who felt it was merely a coincidence. After all, women miscarry frequently. When the natural forces operating within Margarita evolved into the loss of her pregnancy near the third month of her first trimester, she took it rather well. Her friends whispered to themselves that it was Helados's obsession with the dead pelican that aggravated her and caused the loss of the baby. This kind of idea never entered Margarita's mind. She loved Helados too much to blame him for anything. As with all uncertainties, she ascribed the misfortune to God's will.

For Helados, the event was a second omen: a thunderclap, a warning he could no longer avoid. At the time he heard about it, he was working with Sandro at the boat. The morning was waning, and they were late for picking up the first tourists from their hotels. Sandro was annoyed, but he had only himself to blame. The boy that ran up to them was out of breath.

"Margarita is in the hospital. Helados, you must come quickly!"

There was no leave-taking. Helados dropped the oxygen tanks in the boat where he was loading them and ran toward the hospital with the boy. Sandro put both hands on his hips and looked irritated as his friend and worker disappeared into the town.

Helados arrived at the hospital blanched with fear.

The doctor came out to see him, and told him, "Yes, it was a miscarriage, but you need not to worry."

As he heard those words, his mind was in a chaos of other thoughts. The doctor continued speaking, but the sounds passed unwanted into his listener's already trammeled thinking. There was no danger. She could have more children. Why did it happen? There really was no reason. Many women lose a baby on occasion during their fertile years.

"Why are you so distressed?" the doctor asked.

The doctor understood Helados's sadness, but he told him that there was no need to be so worried. Helados felt his back slapped and heard the doctor chuckle.

"Don't worry, Helados. She will have more children for you!"

Helados was unworried about having more children. He was such a good man that he did not concern himself with any other matter but his wife. Once her comfort was secured, he could not avoid delving into the meaning of the pelican's death. It was a strange happening, he thought. The pelican thought everything was as it should be. He dived for his food as he had done hundreds of time before. He expected the sea to be beneath him. He was deceived. Nothing was sure. Helados realized nothing was sure for him as well. Now Margarita lost the baby. What was going to happen next?

To all outward appearances, life returned to normal. Margarita took care of household chores and continued her excellent mothering of their son. Helados went back to work with Sandro. Business was good. Extra trips were added. He was receiving bonuses for extra work, and he was unable to find leisure time to sit on the bench and watch the sea. Nevertheless, his mind churned.

Margarita has changed, he thought. She is not so loving. She too believes the omen has cursed us. My son drops things. There is a spirit in my house. It is a black spirit. How can I trust a black spirit? What do I care if others saw the same bird's death? It looked at me as it drove itself into the beach. The terrible death happened for me to see.

"Oh, Margarita, Margarita!" he cried to himself.

When Margarita saw he was distracted, she tried to comfort him. Since the loss of his baby, his friends had come around more to take him out. Nothing soothed his soul's pain. Every good event was dismissed. The only feeling he felt was foreboding.

He often went to Padre Oscar.

"Helados," the Padre would say to him, "the Virgin blesses you. Why do you remain obsessed with this terrible idea? You have to come to church more often. There is much good fortune in your life. Give up this foolishness."

After these talks, Helados would feel better. He would leave the church smiling.

While lying on his bed one night, just before sleeping, the fear returned. He felt he was lying upon a satin shroud deep in the bottom of a black coffin. He saw his son and wife in coffins next to his. Margarita was next to him, and his son was on his other side. Their eyes were open, but they were not alive. Suspended above them was a skull. It was brilliant-white with ebony black circles around the orbits and a black ellipse around the mouth. In the sockets were large ball eyes that gazed down at him. The mouth opened and closed in such a way that gave the black ellipse the appearance of strangely undulating lips. These lips seemed to castigate him. He was sure he felt it speak. He was sure it warned him to do something, something special and drastic. In this way he might break the curse. The vision terrified him, but it also encouraged him. He now knew there was a way out of his misery. He had been given a solution. He awoke Margarita.

"Are you crazy?" Margarita asked. "Why do you wake me at four in the morning?"

"You must leave the house!" said Helados.

"What? Leave the house? I am not going to leave the house. Go back to bed, Helados. Tomorrow, I will take you to the doctor."

He made her get out of bed and dress herself and their son. Then he ushered them out of the house.

"What are you going to do, you crazy man?"

"I must get rid of the curse. 'The Diablo' will kill us here. There is only one way to rid us of the pelican's omen. Go to the church. Bring Padre Oscar here. I need his blessing for what I must do. Quickly! Go!." His face was unnatural. He was flailing his arms about and jumping frantically. Margarita did not know what to do, but she felt getting Padre Oscar was a good idea. She took her little boy by the hand and ran off to the little house next to the church. After she left, he became busy. He made a great deal of noise. Neighbors turned on their lights and came to their doors to tell him to be quiet. When they got to their doors, because of what they saw, words escaped them.

Margarita and the padre returned to see the same thing. There were two fires. One was for the bed, chairs, tables, clothes, and everything else Helados and his small family owned. The second fire, some twenty feet away to the rear of the first, was the burning of the house itself. Its flames could not be stopped. It was clear to all that Margarita's father's legacy was to be completely destroyed.

"What have you done, Helados?" Margarita cried, pulling at the front of her skirt with her two hands. "You are crazy!" she screamed.

Helados did not go to her. He looked like a man cleansed as he spoke to the padre: "Padre, say a prayer over the loss of my house and my things. Please say a prayer to clean the flames on their way to the sky. Please, Padre. Please!"

Padre Oscar could barely gather his wits enough to agree with his anguished parishioner. He felt awkward as he complied with the pleading man. His words came hesitantly to his lips.

"Blessed are these things that burn. God bless these things. The Father, the Son, and the Holy Ghost bless these things. Amen." Helados smiled. He was sure he saw the white skull disappear in the flames and taken forever by the night sky. He was sure the omen was defeated. He was at peace.

The pleasantly mild, balmy Puerto Vallarta days continued as expected. Helados enjoyed them. All of his anxieties were gone. It saddened him that Margarita refused to live with him. She had been given a room by friends. There she cared for their son and increased her attendance at church. Her feelings toward her husband were mixed, but she could not be with him. He also moved into a room provided by friends. He continued his job with Sandro and gave all his money to Margarita, keeping only the bare minimum for himself. He never saw Lucinta again.

At first, the people of Puerto Vallarta thought Helados was crazy, but when he returned to work and his usual habits, they decided he was not. Some even came to believe he had to do what he did. Who knew all the ways of the world's mysteries, they argued?

Senora Juarez included Helados's story among those she told the young and old who came to her. She could hardly talk; her throat had become raspy and soft since the days of Helados's youthful visits, but it did not diminish her importance to the people who sought her out. Once, a female anthropologist from the University of Virginia recorded her account of the diving pelican. This later became an academic illustration of the Mexican folklore of the region. For many who lived on Bandera Bay, Helados's story was an example of how uncertain life could be. Many in the village stopped watching the pelicans dive. Even in beautiful Puerto Vallarta, a paradise, some said there were fears.

DELIRIUM

He nudged the patient sleeping in the bed before him and said, "Hello. Sorry to wake you. Sorry. I hate to wake sleeping patients, but I have to talk to you."

He nudged him again. The patient stirred and stretched.

"Yes? Who are you?"

"I'm Dr. Martin. I'm the consulting psychiatrist. I have to talk to you."

"Really?" the patient asked. "I'm Dr. Martin. Are we the same person? I don't think so."

"No, not really," the doctor answered. "I'm Dr. Martin, and I've come to interview you."

"Where am I?" the patient asked.

"You're in a hospital, and you're ill. I'm a consultant psychiatrist. I have to ask you a few questions. Sorry to wake you."

The patient mumbled something.

"Yes? What did you say?" the doctor asked.

"Nothing important. You say you're Dr. Martin? You have the same name as I. What is the matter with me?"

"You're in delirium."

"I'm in delirium? Really? How do I know that? How do you know that?"

"Well, I'm a psychiatrist, and I know delirium when I see it."

"How do you know we're not both in delirium?"

The doctor laughed. "Yes, I suppose we could both be, but I'm standing here before you, and I'm going to ask the questions. Will you answer them for me?"

"I can hardly refuse. You're doing my job, except this time you're the doctor, and I'm the patient." He paused. "Am I dying?"

"No, not at all. You have low blood sodium, your blood urea nitrogen is elevated, and there are some minor liver issues. All of these have made you delirious, but I think the medical team can correct them."

"So, I am dying. At least, my death is proximal...or nearly proximal. Yours may be more distal. You are dying too."

"Don't be pessimistic, Robert. You're not dying, just delirious. This proximal–distal thing, however, is interesting. Here's the first question: Where are you?"

"I am in the land of illness and confusion."

"Don't be clever now. I mean, what is the name of this place?"

"I know it's not my house. I know it's not my school. I know I'm in a bed, but the bed could be anywhere. It must be in a place that's normal for beds. How am I doing, Doctor?"

"So, you don't know this is a hospital or the name of the hospital?"

"Oh, of course. I'm in a hospital. I don't think I'm competent. I do think I'm dying. Delirium equals death, no?"

"No, no, not at all. Delirium is not death. Far from it."

"Well then, are you me and am I you? I mean does delirium make all equal. In this sea of my confusion, is some kind of humanitarian equality finally achieved?"

"This has nothing to do with equality, just a doctor and a patient in a consultation."

"Okay. I'm in a hospital. I'm in a bed. I must be ill. I am you and you are me."

"Hardly. We may have the same name, but that does not make us the same. I need to ask though: What day is today?"

"I don't have a clue. There are seven days. This may be any one of them. If you already know I'm in delirium, why are you asking these questions? The answer is before you. I can't answer them. I'm delirious."

"That's true. I suppose I don't need to ask any more questions. The answer is apparent."

"Doctor, may I ask a question?"

"Certainly. What would you like to know?"

"First of all, do you really have the same name as me?"

"Apparently. It's just a coincidence, but still somewhat confusing."

"And you are not delirious?"

The doctor laughed. "No, not at all."

"Then, do you know where you are and what day it is?"

The doctor looked at him and stared blankly. "No. Actually, I don't."

A DOG STORY

Loving a dog may seem trivial to some, but it is not. When Sarah chose Nereid, she was one of three in the litter. At the beginning, she was merely a puppy. When Sarah, then a single girl living in a garage apartment rented from the Reynolds, brought her new dog home, she knew their Rottweiler would be a potential problem. It was. It didn't matter that Nereid was part-Rottweiler herself, the edgy aspect of her breed mix of Rottweiler and Labrador. Whenever Nereid heard the barking other dog, she ran to the couch, buried her head in her paws, and scrunched herself into that cute ball that endears all puppies to their owners.

Nereid started as merely a little companion for Sarah. She peed on the carpet—*bad dog*. She yapped frequently and endeared herself in the unintended ways all puppies do. Sarah loved her for herself. Nereid's job was merely to love Sarah back.

Working at the local newspaper gave Sarah little time for the new dog. However, when she was home, they were inseparable companions. Sarah was not a recluse; she had many friends, and she was a young woman finding herself in the world. The new puppy was an add-on: something she always wanted, important, but not really essential to her life. Still, Sarah and Nereid were a family of two.

Everyone is a little lonely. It is unfair to understate Nereid's importance in those first years of her growth. She naturally matched herself to Sarah's temperament—staying out of the way when Sarah had to type an article and yapping happily when her mistress came home. They adjusted to each other. This is how people and dogs do.

Dogs grow. Is it true they age seven years for every one of a human? Each breed is different, and it's hard to be accurate in these things. In one year, Nereid was fifty pounds, and she started to strain Sarah's back. Nereid was black, sleek, and soft, and in many ways, she was like a sister. Walking her was a challenge as she strained at the leash, pulling toward a squirrel, a pigeon, or a smell. She had amazing speed when chasing something, and Sarah always worried the catch would lead to a death. No one ever taught Nereid, but she could catch a Frisbee midair. Once the disc was thrown, Nereid seemed to be where it would land before it landed, often catching it with her teeth. Her speed and dexterity were a marvel to behold. Many who knew her speculated on her breed being excellent hunters.

She growled at strangers, reluctant to grant anyone sharing rights with her beloved Sarah. This fact made it more surprising when she accepted Gerry without a whimper. Gerry and Sarah began dating earnestly, and Gerry stayed over at the apartment frequently. Gerry and Nereid were often together. Sarah was developing a feeling of love for Gerry, and she jealously wondered why Nereid chose her serious boyfriend over her. This imponderable concern dissolved as the couple grew more serious.

At the wedding, Sarah was pregnant. This was her second with Gerry (the first ended in a miscarriage; they decided to try again, and it happened). Standing at the Hoopa, the Jewish canopy obligated in weddings, was Gerry, Sarah, Sarah's father (who had just given Sarah away), and Nereid. The puppy was now grown and was fully part of the family. Tied around her neck was a spring floral kerchief in pink and lavender. Nereid's behavior was impeccable. She knew, in her own way, what to do, and she did her part well.

Babies sometimes cause adjustment problems for dogs in a family, but not for Nereid. When the little girl came home from the hospital, Nereid took one sniff of the infant and assumed she was family. Nereid never barked at her. Xinny could pull at Nereid, shove her, fall on her, take her food away, or aggravate the animal as toddlers do, but the dog just licked her face. They became very close. Xinny begged to feed her friend when she was three, and the dog waited patiently as the baby awkwardly filled her bowl. Little Xinny would hide the fact that she knew where Nereid's treats were from her mother and would sometimes sneak one to the pet without her mother knowing. It was a family of three.

Gerry took charge of walking Nereid. Every morning he would take her on her constitutional at 5:00 a.m. This became part of his routine and caused some problems in his relationship with Sarah. He would insist on going to bed first, leaving Sarah to take care of the children or watch TV by herself. There were some young marriage fights over this flight from companionship. Gerry would almost always throw in the fact that he had to get up early to take care of Nereid. After some time, both went to opposite sides of the ring and adjusted to the situation. Nereid's walks became a part of the marital compromise.

Sarah loved her dog. Everybody loved her dog. She was part of the family. When they visited the grandparents—who were not especially excited about having a dog shed on their couch or stamp about on their carpets—Nereid came along. Sarah would not entertain talks of leaving her in a kennel. The grandparents loved their daughter, and they would have to love her dog the same way.

The arguments stopped, and the dog was accepted. Sarah could sense that her parents truly became attached to the animal despite initial misgivings.

Xinny began preschool. Xinny asked her mother for a sister over and over. Sarah wanted to give her daughter a sibling, but it turned out to be not so easy. There were problems that had to be solved. Finally, it happened. Melanie became the fourth member of the family. Again, one sniff and Melanie was as accepted by Nereid, just like Xinny was. The dog would sleep either under Melanie's crib or on Xinny's bed. No one understood how the dog that barked at mailmen mercilessly and once bit a little boy who pulled her ears could tolerate the new children in the household. There was an ease of attachment between all four beings in the house. Everyone in the family was a part of the whole. That was just the way it was.

Time passed as it does, and everyone aged. Xinny was due to start the first grade. Melanie was in preschool. Walking Xinny to school every day became a ritual. Nereid, Xinny, Melanie, and Sarah all made the daily trek. All the other children came to know Nereid and Xinny felt comfortable, seeing the attention her dog got.

Gerry had a new job. Sarah was the busy mother of all. She would nuzzle up to Nereid to sleep when the dog was not near the children. At night, when the house was quiet, she noticed the dog had some gray hairs. She had never thought that age would interfere with her attachment. She suddenly realized that Nereid was thirteen. The immediate future pressed itself on to her mind. Everything was as it should be. Why should age mess things up?

The next few months were awful. Aside from bills, children with banged knees or arms, the battles with her temperamental husband (her view), and bills and parking tickets, Sarah gradually began to worry more and more about Nereid.

The dog began staggering. Sometimes the hind leg would drag.

"Perhaps arthritis," the vet declared.

Why was she banging into furniture? Perhaps her vestibular system? What else could go wrong? Well, the dog's kidneys for one. This wonderfully toilet-trained animal was no longer chasing Frisbees and occasionally little accident puddles appeared where none had been before. Sarah was not aggravated. She was concerned.

Many trips to the vet with no clear indications of what was wrong.

"Well, Sarah, she is an old dog," the vet would say.

She was a beloved old dog, a member of the family. In fact, the idea of "dog" began to seem repellent. The more Sarah worried, the more Nereid seemed like a person, someone known since childhood, someone who shared so many family events turned into memories.

"I think her kidneys are failing." Dr. Smithy sounded ominous.

Gerry noticed often that on his walks with her, she wouldn't do her thing.

"Doesn't she have to pee?" he asked rhetorically one night.

"I don't know. What you do you think? Should we consider putting her down? Is she suffering?" Sarah asked.

Sarah was surprised at her own questions. How did she jump so fast mentally from deep abiding love to euthanasia?

"I think it's too early for that," Gerry responded. "What did the vet say the other day?"

Her husband looked glum. He was the strong scientific type.

"We all have to go sometime," he said blithely. Sarah answered by breaking into tears.

She reminded herself the kids were in bed. She could cry profusely without traumatizing them. She did. The usually cool Gerry put his arms around her, and a tear or two appeared on his face. Somehow Sarah felt better.

Sarah hired a home-visiting vet. She wanted someone she could call at a moment's notice. Could the budget cover this extravagance? Who cared? Sarah just wanted to do all she could for her child.

"I think she's good for a while. It's hard to tell with these kidney things. Let's take some blood and find out how she's doing," the visiting vet said.

The numbers were high. There was a creatinine value of 8 and a blood urea nitrogen value of 90, large numbers even for a dog. The kidneys really were not doing their job.

Sarah became distraught, almost unable to take care of her daughters.

"Is Nereid going to die?" Xinny asked.

"We're doing all we can for her. She is very sick."

Xinny persisted: "Is she in pain?"

This was the thought that plagued Sarah. "I don't think so, honey."

Days passed, and the dog began refusing to go out. She would lie on the couch motionless, breathing rapidly. Each day, the children would rub and touch her as if they understood a historic moment in their lives was passing. The visiting vet asked whether Sarah and Gerry felt up to giving Nereid a shot of saline every day. They agreed, but this only increased the sense that they were hurting their family member. On days when Nereid was able to walk, she would avoid them when she thought the injections were coming.

"Are we doing more harm than good?" they asked each other.

The emotional discomfort Sarah felt was beginning to rise to the level of torture. She began obsessing: "Is it better to continue like this or put her down?"

The couple got a babysitter just to get a chance to discuss their predicament. Over pasta and lamb shanks, they tried to remain civil and talk about their options.

"I just want to do the right thing for Nereid. Do you think she's suffering?" She asked again as if for the first time.

This was the pressuring thought she wanted to dispel: "Do you think we should put her down now?"

Gerry hunched his shoulders and, with a deep sigh, said, "Whatever we do, we have to live with it the rest of our lives. We will always come back to this time and ask ourselves if we did the right thing. Wow! This is hard!"

Their love for the dog and their terrible uncertainty of what to expect with its growing inability to function formed the core of their indecisiveness. Everyone watched as the poor animal deteriorated. One morning, Sarah called the vet to come and give an opinion.

He took one look at the dog and said, "It's time."

Sarah was almost relieved, but she also felt this terrible dread of sending her loved one to a destination she understood little of.

"Can we do it tomorrow, Saturday? Sarah asked. "I arranged with a neighbor to take the children. I don't think I want them to see this."

The vet was surprised Sarah had thought ahead and already made arrangements. Clearly, she and Gerry anticipated his words.

"Yes, of course. Will nine o'clock in the morning be all right?"

Sarah spent the night with Nereid. The children had gone to bed after hugging their pet. Gerry went to bed also, promising to be there in the morning. Sarah felt a little abandoned by him, but she had grown used to his handling this his own way. They didn't fight over his decision. Ordinarily, they would have. They didn't have much fight left in them, after the past few weeks. Nereid was breathing rapidly, but nothing could be done.

"Respiratory acidosis," the vet had said. "The kidneys are just not adjusting the pH of the blood anymore. It's too acidic."

At this point Sarah cared little of the acid–base balance of the blood. She only wanted to hug her dear friend forever. She fell asleep while crying and hugging her companion.

The next morning, everything happened as if time had sped up. The vet came. Each child stroked Nereid's paw and hugged her before they went dutifully to Sarah's friend, the neighbor down the street. The children were saying goodbye, but the enormity of the meaning of that seemed to escape them. Only later would they place their own interpretation on this momentous event. Once the children left, Sarah hugged Nereid again.

Gerry held Nereid in his arms as the vet injected the potent solution into the animal. Nereid's limbs went limp and the ordeal found its culmination.

A sudden emptiness filled the room.

* In loving memory of Neisha

THE PARTY

My friend was not so much like Jay Gatsby as he was a caricature of him. His parties were not as frequent and they were not consistently as lavish. Yet there I was, with Sarah, on a flight from Long Island to Puerto Vallarta, with a stop at Mexico City. His invitation to a Gatsby-like, high-life 50th birthday bash for himself could not be ignored.

Quite frankly, I live on the conservative side. I'm out of character when I leave my neurology practice to fly to Mexico just for a birthday celebration. The fare was not cheap. Even though he was paying for the hotel, the food, the entertainment, and airport transportation connections, I ordinarily would not have been enticed. Yet he was my old childhood friend. I had not seen him for a long time. I'm a sucker for nostalgia. Also, I could not put aside the other reason: the idea of a friend of mine being able to pay for 128 people for a weekend suggested this would be an event of proportion and quality I could not let pass me by.

His name was not really Carlyle Phillips. I once asked him where he got that name. He laughed and said he didn't know. It just came to him. He liked the sound of it. There were a lot of *ls* which made the tongue pause under the palate, and so on. He wasn't anti-Semitic; he simply thought Hymie Udersky was a bit much for a social climber. He always gave his occupation as "an aspiring member of the financial elite."

I could never think of old Hymie as Carlyle. Once, I met him sporting a gold-headed cane and a moustache, as if he walked through the frame of a gilded age portrait. On that day he wore a perfectly pressed gray suit and vest, adorned with a red silk tie blazing off his white silk shirt.

"Hymie," I said, "I can't believe it's really you."

We both laughed. When he was with me, his pretentions always melted. To him, I was always Sam Rubino, his Italian friend from the old block in Brooklyn.

I married a Jewish girl. My parents went crazy. Her parents went crazy. Elope? No. We considered it, but the families came around. Both sets were wise and educated, fully aware of what happened between the Montagues and Capulets. We were married by Rabbi Kingsly, after a coin flip where rabbi trumped priest. I add these personal details because I want you to appreciate Hymie's part in my life. He was there for me and Sarah. While the very educated parents fumed, he metaphorically held our hands and planned our escape with us. He knew a cargo ship captain who would do him a favor. Relieved our parents capitulated, we didn't have to indulge in his wild idea.

Another wild idea of his always came forth at cocktail parties. One drink and he would be off with the notion that people were on earth as repositories for viruses. He would postulate that viruses were not mere bugs that caused colds, AIDS, or a change in the gene pool, but were natural inhabitants of the plant that used us humans.

"We came on earth to supply the viruses the hosts they required," he would say. "If they get mad at us, we will pay."

He would then gesticulate the gory possibilities of viruses seeking revenge on the human species.

"They are not alien forms; we are!"

The exclamation usually got a reaction. I thought he was verging to an obsession with this idea because he brought it up so often in those days.

Puerto Vallarta Airport was a madhouse in February. The high season delivered a room of densely packed tourists wiggling and swirling to avoid the almost equal number of diminutive swarthy Mexicans carrying their suitcases. Amidst the bustle, we spied the man holding our "Dr. and Mrs. Rubino card." He was wearing a white suit with a white tie, grinning broadly when he saw we recognized him.

"Dr. and Mrs. Rubino, it is a pleasure to meet you. The limousine is waiting. Mr. Phillips and I hope you had a comfortable journey. Please come with me."

Aside from the emphasis he placed on "doctor," he seemed sincere and pleasant. His Spanish accent was strong, suggesting Catalan parents from old Spain. Sarah and I looked at each other pleased and fondly accepted the obsequious reception.

"Can you imagine? A white limousine?" Sarah whispered as we drove away from the airport. "Are we in a dream sequence of Fantasy Island—white suit, white car?"

Hymie's excessive style was tickling. Senor Hernandez was driving, and he urged us to have a drink from the bar.

"Please call me Rico, Senor."

I paused and said, "Doesn't that mean 'rich' or 'tasty' as in food?"

I saw him smile in the mirror.

"*Si*, Senor Doctor, you are correct."

I did not pursue the matter. Instead, I decided to find out a little more about him.

"Senor Hernandez—"

"Please, Senor Doctor, call me Rico. I like that better," he interrupted.

"OK, Rico. We haven't seen Senor Phillips for some time. What business is he into now?

He replied eagerly: "Well, the senor is into real estate. He owns two villas here in Mexico. I think he owns more in the United States and at least one property in Europe. The other day he mentioned South African gold mines, but he might not have been talking about himself."

I was puzzled as I recalled Hymie swearing, he would never do real estate.

"You mean he sells villas?"

After turning the wheel to avoid a goat in the road, Rico said, "I think so, Senor Doctor. Anyway, I can tell you he is a very generous man. You know this. You are his friend, yes?"

I answered that I was and dropped the conversation.

The white limousine and white-clad Rico drove up to the Grand Regency Hotel. I couldn't believe even the wealthy Hymie was putting up so many people in such an expensive place, but there he was on the steps to welcome us.

His moustache was gone, and he was wearing a Florida flowered shirt and short pants. His ear-to-ear grin matched Rico when he saw us, except Hymie followed up with his usual Jewish bear hug.

As soon as the welcoming was finished, he turned to me with sad eyes and said, "Sammy, the hotel screwed me. It's overbooked. I'm really sorry. I have made arrangements for my guests at the Fiesta Hotel. I just found out. I didn't want you and Sarah to discover this at the desk. Please forgive me. Rico will take you to the Fiesta at once. I have some haggling to do here. I'll see you at the party. Is that alright?"

"You dressed yet? Sarah yelled at me from the bathroom where she was finishing with her hair.

"Just waiting for you," I answered. "It's eight o'clock. We're going to be late for Hymie's 50th after all this. Can't you hurry? It's not really fair to be late."

Her silence told me she was miffed. Within seconds, she emerged.

"Don't push me," she said and scowled. "The beginning of these things is always slow. We're only upstairs. It shouldn't take us five minutes to get to the veranda."

She was right. In less than three minutes, we were seated. Excited by the expectations of grand festivities, we implicitly agreed to bury our annoyance at each another. Hymie came over to the table. He repeated his bear hug, and we wished him a wonderful birthday with considerable sincerity. He sent an upgraded bottle of champagne to our table, better than the ones other guests received. Our cemented bond warmed us and put us completely under his spell. It was a wonderful evening.

With the dinner over and dancing from the talented Mariachi band completed, we were told the fireworks were beginning. All 128 people walked toward the beach, clearly intoxicated by the starlit Mexican sky. The dim shadowy shabbiness of the Fiesta Hotel became lost in the romantic, cool, and delicate Puerto Vallarta night. The full orb of the bright moon gave vision to the crested soft waves wafting onto the beach. Sarah and I felt inexplicably and romantically completely alone.

Hymie stood at the very edge of the beach, dressed in his tuxedo and a portable microphone in hand. We all faced him, looking at him and the water beyond.

"Thank you, my dear friends, for letting me entertain you. It means much to me that you gave of your time and money to join me for this occasion. Each of you is special to me, and you fill me with memories of our experiences together. In honor of that and more, here are the fireworks!"

Immediately, the black sky, embraced by the full moon, broke into a volcano of organized fire. The pyrotechnics came from five boats jogging through the waves. In the center was a huge rectangle ablaze with color spelling out "HAPPY BIRTHDAY, HAPPY 50th, CARLYLE PHILLIPS." On either side of this display were twirling rockets with sirens, vertical shooting spears with blue and red colors trailing behind. Comets reached their vertical peaks and exploded, shedding thousands of minute drops of lighted particles that sprinkled down onto the water and disappeared. White, green, purple, and vermillion fireworks exploded in a riot of deafening sound. The entire extravaganza seemed to last more than half an hour. I squeezed Sarah's hand. This was impressive.

The sounds died away, and the lights disappeared. We were left with the disappearing moon and the dark sky.

Hymie, now invisible but presumably still on the beach, reached beyond the still moment to say, "Thank you, my friends. Have a wonderful trip home. I love you all. Thank you for loving me. Good night."

⇥⊹⊱

Sarah and I took a few days to come back to ourselves. Our hotel bill was paid. Hymie really came through. There was some talk at the party whether he could handle this expense. Many jokes alluded to the return of truth at checkout.

"Well, just in case, I've got my American Express card," many laughingly offered.

There turned out to be no reason for concern. We left paying no more than our airfare. That was it. Hymie had indeed put on and paid for a spectacularly good show.

It was eleven o'clock two weeks later when the phone rang. We were reading in bed when the voice announced it was Melvin Saperstein.

"Hello, Sam, how are you?"

Puzzled, I said, "I'm fine, Mel. What's up?"

Sleep is what I wanted after a particularly hard day, not a cheery late conversation.

"I need a donation for Hymie," Mel said.

I sat up, rattling Sarah's composure with my abrupt excitement. "Why does Hymie need a donation? That doesn't make sense."

Saperstein was not to be put off. "Yeah, Hymie's in a Mexican jail. Remember our party, it turned out he couldn't pay the bill. He tried every credit card he had, but they didn't work. Then the hotel wanted cash. He bargained, he promised, but in the end, they called the police and had him put in jail. Do you know what a Mexican jail is like?"

Every time I responded to Mel, Sarah repeated what I said. I said "jail," and she said "jail," and so on.

"So, how much did the party cost him?"

Mel knew: "$32,000."

I slowly answered: "Well, from what I saw around Hymie—his villas, his servants, the way everyone kowtowed to him—I would think he could dig up $32,000. He could sell a villa."

Mel pleaded, "I think he is planning to sell one, but the Mexicans are ruthless. They think he is a sheik. They expected immediate cash payment. When they saw his American Express card had expired, they really got pissed."

I thought for a moment and then said, "Alright, Mel, count me in. Figure out what the group is going to contribute and tell me how much you need from me."

After all, Hymie was my friend.

I never heard from Mel about this again. A week or so later, I met Peter Lublin. He told me there was a question as to whether Hymie was really in a Mexican jail. Mel was not a liar. He simply may have been misled by what he learned from Rico, Hymie's major-domo. Peter learned from Milly, Hymie's ex-lover who was also at the party, that Hymie really couldn't pay the bill.

"She said he had used his charm to talk the hotel into waiting a week, guaranteeing cash for their patience. She is not sure, but she thinks Hymie is in the Black Forest at a resort in Germany," Peter explained.

"So why did Mel call me for a donation?" I asked.

Peter didn't know for sure.

"Maybe it was a scam Hymie set up?" he queried.

We met our friend Milly at the supermarket a few days later. It was one of those unexpected meetings. We hardly ever saw Milly. She called to us while we were at the checkout line with groceries suitable for a month.

"Hi!" she squealed.

She was dressed in one of those leopard jackets no woman should be seen in, and she brandished multiple wrist bracelets that rang out loudly with every gesture as if she was in the percussion section of an orchestra. She was always a bit unnerving to me, but this time, within the hubbub of the Food Emporium, she was particularly abrasive. We exchanged pleasantries, and I made the best of the situation by asking her about Hymie. She suddenly looked somber.

"I don't know where he is," she moaned. "He was supposed to call me. It's not so expensive from Germany. Have you heard from him?"

I replied that I hadn't and asked her what might be going on. I admit my tone was a little accusatory.

"Going on? What do you mean 'going on'?"

She was accusatory right back. I explained about Saperstein's phone call and told her I was puzzled. I softened everything by finishing with my concern about Hymie and how much I would want to help him if he were in trouble.

"Well, why ask me?" She seemed genuinely offended. "I haven't seen him since the party. You know we don't see each other so much anymore, don't you? As far as I know, he is in Germany. Hymie's a screwball, but he wouldn't do anything mean."

Soon after, Rico called. He was in the United States, in San Diego, or so he said.

"Did you send money to Senor Saperstein?" he queried.

I replied, no. He then suggested that if I wanted to help Senor Phillips, I should send the money not to Mel but to the Mexican jail in Puerto Vallarta. He gave me a specific name and address. I asked him about my hearing that Hymie was in Germany. He said that was ridiculous. Hymie was still in jail and needed $28,000 to get out. When I told him I heard it was $32,000 and that I had a personal conversation with Milly who told me our friend was in the spa area of Germany, somewhere in the vicinity of Baden-Baden. He said I was being misled. Suddenly, his accent was diminished, and he spoke very clear English.

"You should only deal with me regarding something as important as Mr. Phillip's life."

Sarah and I began to feel very guilty. We had fed off Hymie's friendship. He may be in serious trouble. Though the details were confusing, we did want to help. We cared for our friend a great deal. Not only had he stood beside us during our religious family strife, he also provided us with a relationship that was unique and stimulating. It was unthinkable that he might disappear into the bowels of the Mexican penal system.

Trying to get our heads around the contradictions seemed challenging. Was he imprisoned or not? Before we sent money, Sarah constrained me and insisted we should find out more. I located the jail address Rico had provided. I took a chance and telephoned the number attached to the address. Sarah stood next to me as I dialed.

"Hello. Hello!" I shouted. Long distance and another language left me with the illusion that if I yelled in broken English, somehow, I would be better understood.

"Is Senor Phillips in *su* jail?"

My terrible Spanish was unnecessary. Tourism had done its job.

"No, Senor, he was here, but he is not here now."

Yes, Hymie was out. It was wonderful of the Mexicans not to stand on ceremony with me.

The policeman told me what I wanted to know. Hymie's ordeal was over. Now, however, the plot gathered in mystery. Sarah and I spent the night speculating over what really happened. Even our two twenty-one-year-old fraternal twins got into the act. They had this believable theory: Hymie was part of a cocaine ring; he owed money on a confiscated shipment, and the police matter was a total scam to get immediate funds to pay his connections.

We never found out. The cocaine idea never proved true; or, at least, there was never any evidence to support it. Rico called once more for money and then stopped. A letter came from Hymie with German postage on it. Milly wasn't so daffy about his geographical peregrinations. We then got another letter from Rico wishing us well as if he merely wanted to maintain contact. His letter didn't mention money. Hymie's letter also left payment out. He was fine. Our gift for his birthday was wonderful. He said he would see us soon.

Two years have passed. Some friends that we shared with Hymie came over for dinner recently. Carlyle Phillips dominated our conversation. After much babble about the party and Hymie's incarceration, a consensus emerged that Hymie, the gambler and wheedler, had found his bill too large. He had hoped he would recoup some of his loss by having Rico call Mel and making Mel a dupe to swindle his friends. The friends had enjoyed the party; why not pay some of it back? Perhaps Hymie was living closer to the edge than everyone had guessed. He had not expected Milly to tell about the trip to Germany. He was never in jail, but Hymie could talk anyone into almost anything. It seems he may well have had a close relationship with the Mexican police. So, when I called, the guards just earned their payola. Rico had called to cover the entire trick. It was too late. At that point, everyone was feeling suspicious enough not to readily pass him money across the border. We agreed that $1,000 a couple would have been reasonable. We would have paid that if the story were true.

All this explaining was conjectural speculation. As of this writing, Carlyle Phillips has not been seen. None of our acquaintances know where he is. He is a wonderful source of conversation. His party, indeed, goes on and on. We had a wonderful time at my old friend's expense, and we still do. Our affection is strong, our sense of being fooled awhile is pleasurable, and he accentuates our ordinary daily lives with his humor and guile.

"Where is he?" Sarah asked me one night before we turned off the bed light. "Do you think the viruses have gotten him?"

MEETING AT THE PIERRE

Phyllis Kallan rested against the taxi seat, somewhat surprised to find herself there. She was on route to her first rendezvous since the death of her husband fifteen years ago. She was the consummate passenger—ignoring how the Uber driver maneuvered in and out of bus lanes and oblivious of the other Manhattan vehicles threatening her and her driver's lives. Even the jerking, which defied comfort by arresting her and the car in forward motion, did not disturb. Her mind was elsewhere.

Everything about her was in transition. She was passing from the gray gloom of depression into a recent decision to "get on with it." This depression held her in zombie-like suspension for these fifteen years, and only the past month began to weaken its hold. She asked herself when the weakening happened. Perhaps it was during group therapy. The therapist was good. Phyllis felt the woman was professional (reasonably caring in the world of therapy). She ran the group well enough so that the issues Phyllis suffered were addressed.

The therapist once said, "Losing your companion after fifteen years is difficult. You could live next to a rock and feel the loss if it was taken away. Losing a lover and a person who shares life with you is so much more difficult."

The taxi came to a stop, and the thought came back to her. Yes, she thought, Howard wasn't perfect but he was better than a rock, and I miss him. Her ride started up again.

As the gloom dissipated and her friends noticed, they began urging her to do something about being isolated for so long. The singles scene in New York for sixty-year-olds must rank as one of the most arduous and difficult of the mating Olympics. She couldn't get started until somebody handed her a card. Ellen handed her the card, she remembered. The card read, "LPB."

"You're not guaranteed anything," Ellen exclaimed, "but the Loving Persons' Bureau has been good for me."

Phyllis looked at her doubtfully.

"OK, I know you're thinking I've not met anyone, but the guys I've dated via the LPB have been, ah, acceptable."

Ellen was not only a good friend, but she had acquired the credential of being a decent judge of men. This was just enough for Phyllis to take the card and call the number on it. LPB sounded inane, but she felt she needed this life change, so she telephoned.

The Loving Persons' Bureau was banal and officious. She had expected leather seats and assorted flowers. She had difficulty seeing with the overly bright lights, the standard office decor with a lot of chrome. Her immediate guide to hopeful expectations was a woman in her forties, who was attractive and was dressed in a jacket and buttoned blouse accented by a flowery cravat. A matching foulard draped her shoulder as in the French style.

"Chic, at least," Phyllis concluded. As she spoke there was a slight swell to her gestures—like sea waves coming to soothe then receding to the ocean, leaving the feeling that there must be more. She had a glow, an aura of sexual success announcing she did not suffer the deprivations of her clients. Phyllis admired the narrow waist of a careful youth, her full breasts, and her undoubtedly dyed blond hair. Clearly, Ms. Gerund knew men. The overall effect had Phyllis resenting the show of success and feeling a kind of social sadism oozing from Ms. Gerund's extended hand.

Introductions over, Ms. Gerund announced the file.

"Here is our choice of men in your age group who fit the requirements you gave us. You can use room 2B down the hall. Take your time."

"All of these guys are looking for a sixty-year-old?" Phyllis joked.

"You'd be surprised."

The impressive blond smiled and waved her hand toward 2B.

Phyllis and her Uber ride moved closer to the assignation. She could not help reflecting on the marginal nature of her current adventure. She had sent out fourteen mailings based on the initial perusal of what she fondly found herself calling "The Notebook." From these fourteen, she received no response. None. Nada. The swallowing of her pride and the investment of $1,200 seemed to do nothing to make men want to meet her. A conference was called.

"We have a suggestion for you, but you must promise not to be offended."

It was Ms. Gerund again. Phyllis wanted to ask about her name which suggested a noun turned into a verb, but she didn't think the blond had the wit to enjoy the joke. She always prided herself on handling directness and truthful facts.

"Go ahead," said Phyllis.

"Why don't you redo the video?"

She felt clerical kindness whisked across the space between them. She remembered the kind she used to see her Mother Superior exhibit in Catholic school when the cowl-clad warrior admonished her for her short skirt in junior high school. The good part was the nun looked like Grace Kelly, and this softened the critical blow.

"Redo the video?" Phyllis was now playing uncertain to draw out the viewpoint of the "gerund" blond.

"Yes…well, we don't think you're going to be successful acting like the city intellectual."

"We?"

"We do confer on how to help our clients. This is one opinion that surfaced."

Of course, she remade the video. The coaching cost her $1,200 and guaranteed three takes. Her dark, sultry beauty born from her Italian parentage had dissipated. The two-colored drabness of her days of depression affected her couture. She had depended on her keen mind and her working companions' regards. Appearance was forgotten for chagrin. She was the thin, wiry woman whose confidence in many years in the advertising world carried all the weight that was needed. Now, in the social world of dating and meeting (the world of impressions and looks), she seemed to her eye ill-fitted and awash with sartorial blah. There was no value placed on sober-minded persuasiveness. The essence of maturity lost significance. The "please like me" reality of the New York social scene was the password for hunting for a companion.

The video was released. She got a bite: Phillipe Venteux. He liked what he saw. The second try worked. The meeting was arranged. The Pierre Hotel was the rendezvous point. A try assignation. She was excited. His email included the hotel address. She began having doubts: Why a hotel address? Was he an employee? Should she go? The situation was so ambiguous. There was this giddy feeling, a strange excitement she could only place in her adolescence. Yes. What did she have to lose besides her depression? Just the idea titillated. She couldn't help herself.

Her thoughts leaned toward the ballroom scene in an opera. She quickly caught herself. Reality would be different. Besides, she had no intentions of buying a gown for a first meeting. She was going to give it a try. Maybe a cocktail dress. Maybe something would come out of it. Maybe.

God, I'm sixty, she thought. Howard died fifteen years ago. When you're dead, you're REALLY dead. She emphasized "really" in her thoughts. There was no telephone call, no shaking, nothing that could bring him back. He wasn't without flaws. He coughed when he began to speak. He sometimes picked at his nose. He could be quite dominating. The glow of the marriage had not gone out when he got that infection. The hospital killed him. He should have never gone in. Maybe he'd be alive today if he had been treated at home. She welled up with a tear and caught herself. Whatever his faults, it was twenty years of adapting and enjoying, and suddenly she was alone for fifteen years.

He was good at managing. The advertising agency was quite a success, and there was no concern over money. Sam took it over. She didn't care. Let her son have the excitement. She was too busy mourning to run things. He was doing a decent job. Business floundered but bounced back. At the moment it was out of the mud. At least, it paid for her apartment on Madison. That was something. Cara was well-compensated. The siblings seemed to get along.

She saw the elegant hotel before the taxi stopped. It was a cool evening. Her Hermès shawl adequately covered her singing dress iridescence into the night air. She felt in tune with the moment. She paid the driver and added a nice tip. The doorman extended an arm to the front door and, with the other, closed the car door behind her.

"Thank you," she said.

She brushed through the front door. She was committed. She felt good and smart, dressed in a way she had neglected for such a long time. The single-piece dress decorated her outside of her usual style. The sweater and skirt of her daily life were left at home. She dared to wear Howard's 10th anniversary gift: a necklace of interlocking gold chain links. The light-green dress was complimented. She smiled as she considered the $200-prepared hair atop her head. It was a special night. Phyllis knew she looked smart and felt ready for whatever happened.

Consider that she was a Greenwich Village intellectual; she was well-read, and was at the top of her mental game. Against character, she was worried about her facade, the empty female presentation that might capture a male's heartless eye. Painting, books, and music were her métiers. Glowing in a sexual encounter had never been her inclination. She believed a person's character was the essence of what was important about them. Impressions, appearance, and style were all good for the young social enthusiast, but it always seemed shallow and meaningless to her. Here she was, in the fashionable Pierre, waiting eagerly for her man of the moment in an expensive dress, a well-coiffed hair, and a strange inner trembling to be found satisfactory by the other gender. Why should she not be pleased by being *de rigueur*? Hell. Enjoy the moment, she told herself as the mirror on the hotel wall told her she looked rather splendid. Her gray and black appearance had dissolved into color, and she refused not to be pleasured by the whole thing.

"Mrs. Phyllis Kallan?" a voice said.

She looked toward the soft and mellifluous voice. The inquiry was reasonable, but it broke through her reverie like a thunderclap. She focused on the image of the man before her.

This soft intrusion was dapper. He was dressed in a fine suit, clearly worn for the evening to impress her. He brandished a light-pink handkerchief in his breast pocket that matched the pink shirt caressed by his black jacket. She began to laugh as she took in his handlebar tapered moustache. The laugh was held back in concerned containment. The moustache was long and narrow. At each end of the waxed hair, the turned-up artifice reminded her of double exclamation points symmetrically indenting his cheeks. The emerging thought was that he was ridiculously looking too much like Salvador Dali. Restraint was becoming more difficult.

She had been sitting on a hall divan while waiting for him. He came punctually, and she remarked to herself that this was a man who would not be late. From this first impression, she sensed his overall presentation was imposed upon with too great an intent. She, of course, might be blamed for the same thing. This was a night when each was to make a mark on the other. She was not displeased. The man was interesting: the lobby, a compliment; and the meeting, a welcomed change. She was fully prepared to be swept away.

"Yes. You must be Phillipe Venteux?"

This was the immediate reply she blurted while looking straight at him with no dismay or demure. She wondered how her age may affect him. He did seem younger. Fifty-three? She felt this urge to speak in a cynical New York way about the meeting, but she held back again. She really did want this to go well. Her behavior was that of a woman of the city charmed to be met. As a result, every-thing at the moment sparkled and approached enchantment.

Phillipe guided her into the warm June night. He stood still. Following his movements as if being led onto a dance floor, she stopped as he did. He poised for a decision, or, at least, it seemed so. She waited. The decision wafted away somewhere, and she saw for the first time there was no moon. The park was quite dark.

He looked at her and said, "I'll get a taxi. Can you stand here a moment?"

She sensed a strange ambivalence over getting a ride, but she merely answered, "Certainly. Of course."

She watched in increasing discomfort as he repeatedly tried to hail a cab and wondered why he didn't simply use an Uber app. She thought of offering her own but decided against it. Wednesday at half past six in the evening in New York, she knew, was a very dif-ficult time to get a ride. It was as if the entire city of livery drivers caught his insincere and reluctant inclinations and decided not to stop. He was, it appeared, passed en masse.

He returned to her, saying, "Excuse me, Phyllis."

"Yes?" she replied sweetly, almost like a teenager at the prom.

"Would you very much mind taking a bus?"

He gallantly took her arm and led her to Madison Avenue, a block away. There, waiting like a limousine, was the number four bus. Puzzlement began to swell inside her. This "Beau Brummel" from the Pierre was taking her on a bus? Well, the taxis wouldn't stop. Why not Uber? Why not just eat at the Pierre? Doubts ran through her mind, rapidly crashing into one another.

The massive city vehicle bounced in and out of the potholes of Madison Avenue as it passed the expensive boutiques, wine stores, and well-known shops. She wondered about walking, but she had no idea where he was bound. Until now he had not said a word about the evening and his plans. She soon realized they could have walked on this rather pleasant night, as the bus had barely passed two stops when he indicated their arrival. He stepped out the door first and turned to help her descend the two-foot rise above the sidewalk. As her foot hit the pavement, she saw her destination before her: Leo's Restaurant. Leo's?

Phyllis was beside herself. A peculiar feeling swelled within. This was funny...really funny. She felt the tug of pretentious displeasure nagging at her own internal duplicity. Arrogance was not her inclination, but she was feeling arrogance nevertheless. Would anyone fail to compare the hotel where she was with the establishment where she would dine? She knew Leo's quite well. She often met friends there for breakfast or lunch. She liked the salads. Consternation became her mood and deception her plan. She fought off the pretentious displeasure she felt from coming down from her fancied elegance. She looked again at her escort and played with his name. She changed it from Phillipe—with the accent on the last syllable elongating the *e* in the French style—to Phillip, with the accent on the first syllable as any American would say it. So, she thought, sarcastically, Phillip from the Pierre has taken me to Leo's on Madison in the magnificence of conventional dating. Interestingly, Phillipe suspected nothing. His mind was clearly encased in Saran Wrap. He had his own idea of what this evening was to be. He was true to himself. Her feelings were not under consideration. They were irrelevant. He believed his plan was unfolding as it should. He held the restaurant's door for her to enter.

He quickly passed her, a little abruptly and forcefully, to say to the maître d', "Two please?"

Phyllis almost cackled but held back. The maître d' was, in fact, Leo's cousin, and he was clearly filling in tonight. He blandly picked up two large plastic menus and conducted Phyllis and Phillipe to a table. He didn't seem to care that his two guests were overdressed for the occasion. Maybe he did notice as he gave them the modest restaurant's nicest table in the corner, near the window looking over Madison Avenue.

"Enjoy your dinner," he said with a slight cock of his head as if he did represent a distinguished establishment.

Dinner was calming. With the cat largely out of her companion's bag, she began to enjoy what she had. She complied with Phillipe's suggestion that she get the bluefish special, and it turned out to be quite good. She, of course, knew about the bluefish from previously dining at Leo's. She suddenly realized that Phillipe had brought her to his favorite place.

When the timely space between the main course and dessert came, she couldn't tolerate the mystery of her companion any longer.

"What do you do, Phillipe?"

"I work at the Pierre."

"What do you do there?"

"I'm security."

"Security?"

Phyllis had to ask short questions after every short reply. She recalled how she once wanted to teach kindergarten.

"I'm a guard there."

"Oh!" She uttered a soft "oh," not a startled "oh." She didn't want to abuse the man.

To her surprise, he did go on without prompting: "I've been at the Pierre for eleven years."

Boyish enthusiasm crossed his face. Pride emerged.

"Eleven years? Interesting," she said, as if she was an interviewing social worker. There was no judgment in her voice.

Leo's cousin unceremoniously dropped the large plastic-wrapped menus on the table for them to choose dessert. Phillipe scrutinized the menu with the intentional passion of a serious collector. After a long two minutes, or so it seemed, he chose apple pie à la mode and urged her to pick something. Despite his overeager beckoning, she passed. She did succumb to Leo's cousin's urging to take a cup of decaf, grateful for something warm to place her hands around.

He had his pie, and she had her coffee.

Then he spoke again with no prodding: "Phyllis?"

"Yes." She could not bring herself to speak his name.

"I must be honest with you. I'm married."

"You are?!"

She surprised herself. She would have been angry if her interest in this man had developed. It had not, and she was not. She did feel misled, and her unexpected verbal explosion was based on the unexpected quality and timing of his confession. Her expectations were dashed, her fantasies crushed, and her hope for release from the loneliness after Howard's death prolonged. Who or what Phillipe was had little to do with her reaction. His betrayal was everything. The surprises of the evening caught up with her. It was the inaccurate anticipation that drove the eruption from her heart. She felt no remorse over the failed assignation, only disappointment. As she recovered, she wondered if he would pay the bill.

"I'm married, but I like you, Phyllis. I'm willing to compromise."

"You are?" She replied with complacent resignation but was considering what a duplicitous fool this man truly was.

"Yes. You see. I find you interesting. I think you're intelligent. The dating service doesn't come up with intelligent women very often. I really think you're smarter than me, but men, I know, are hard to find. Aren't they?"

She noticed the more he spoke, the more common he seemed. She was ticking off his grammatical errors in her mind.

"Yes," she reluctantly muttered, almost in a whisper, almost disgruntled.

She suddenly realized he might misinterpret her "yes." She didn't for a moment want him to think she was agreeing with him. Her midwestern style could be misleading. She was bred to be polite. Even the hotel, the bus, Leo's, and Phillipe himself could not break her. Probity until the very end, she thought.

"Well, you see. I'm willing to compromise. I need love. I think we could be good together. Don't you?"

Her soul awakened. She almost called him Leo; she was so distracted by his crass presumption.

"Look, Phillip"—she pronounced his name in the American style she felt it deserved—"I don't think I would ask you to compromise. I am looking for…ah…something a little different."

She wondered to herself why she was being so nice, sparing his feelings. Her current thought was he was a boob. She decided that hurting him or showing him her disappointment had little value.

"I certainly would not have misled you," she continued tenderly.

He, of course, entirely missed the double entendre. She meant for him not to see it, but was bemused by her expectation proving correct.

"I'm not inclined toward the offer you made. I hope you will understand."

He looked sad and looked caught by his own petard.

"That's too bad. I had hoped for more. I find so many women want marriage. Why is that?"

She could not believe his question. The teacher in her held her growing impatience in check.

"I think a woman needs commitment." Hoping this admission was not too big for him, she went on: "It isn't necessarily marriage."

"Oh."

He fell silent. His debonair manner disappeared. He began to slump just a little. He was hurt. In the topsy-turvy world caused by his psychological stupidity, he felt the victim and was incapable of seeing what he had done to her. He felt turned down, rejected, and acknowledged to himself that keen disappointment that all his efforts were wasted, his investment coming to naught. The ends of his moustache still held erect like pillars left over from a previously bold civilization. An intolerable and uncomfortable feeling arose between the couple. Phyllis felt it was time to leave.

With relief, she saw him pay the check. She could have paid it, but she felt to her core that he should. What he thought about this was hidden. With his wallet ensconced in his pants' back pocket, he came over to help her get out of her chair.

"I hope you enjoyed the meal?"

"Yes," she replied gently. "The bluefish was rather good. Thank you for recommending it."

As they approached the door, he said, "Are you taking a cab home?"

"Well, I thought I might."

"Do you mind if I ride a part of the way with you?"

She did not reply to this, merely continuing through the door. She knew he expected her to pay for the taxi, and he planned to take a little advantage to compensate himself psychologically. She elected to keep her annoyance to herself reminding herself that caution at this point was sensible.

Stepping into the street, she quickly and successfully waved down a taxi while he stood leaning casually on a lamp post. When the car stopped, he held the door for her as she got in.

At 69th and 5th Avenue, he asked the cab to pull over. He got out and stood on the street leaning into the cab through Phyllis's open window.

"It was nice meeting you, Phyllis. I'm sorry we could not do something together."

Putting the signature to his sentence, she responded, "Again, thank you for dinner."

He pulled away from the car and walked into the moonless night.

When the taxi took her to her apartment, she gave the driver his fare plus a large tip. She felt a bit of generosity to someone was in order.

Entering the building, she could not prevent a smile. The smile broke into an audible laugh. Cara was waiting for her.

"How'd it go?" her daughter eagerly asked, all bubbly.

"I can't wait to tell you," Phyllis replied.

FREE WILLY

Jeremy didn't want to go to the movies. Neither did Adria. *Free Willy* was excessively banal for two teenagers. I wanted to go. It was about orcas, it was in technicolor, and I'd had enough fighting with my soon-to-be ex-spouse for one day. The theater was not far away, just a ten-minute car ride. I knew Willy would take my mind off my troubles. My children may have thought the movie was not for them; they were too old for it. I wasn't. I needed a break.

Queens's traffic extended the planned ten minutes to twenty. Then I had to park. Coming around the same corner for a second time, I saw a spot. I could still get to the movie, I thought, as I pulled in with minimum effort. Yes, I knew how to park a car. At the moment of self-congratulation, I saw her come out of the now dark alley.

I was an EMT, and I knew an emergency when I saw one. She staggered, she fell. The waning light was too soft to make out much else. The car was already off, and I jumped out to go to the woman. Her wig, the mark of her Jewish orthodoxy, had fallen to the ground. It doesn't take long for the thought to go through the brain: What was an orthodox woman doing unaccompanied, falling in a dark alley? The bruises were extensive. Someone, I bet it was a male, beat her severely. She was conscious, but she could only moan a mixture of Yiddish and English.

I knelt over her, looking at her wounds and trying to determine if I needed to apply resuscitation.

A bystander came by, and I yelled out, "Call 911, now!"

She remained awake, but she was clearly in terrible pain. Perhaps she had a fracture. Judging from the degree of the beating, it would not have surprised me. Still, despite the feeling of desperately wanting to do something, there was little I could do to help besides stay by her side and wait for an ambulance.

The police came first, asking, "What happened here? Were you fighting? The ambulance is on its way, maybe seconds. Are you all right?"

There was no waste of words here: "I am fine. No, there was no fight with me. I saw her coming out of that alley barely able to stand up. I came to help and told someone standing by to call 911. I don't even know who called."

"I did," a voice sounded and then disappeared forever.

In the middle of these brief sentences, the ambulance arrived. The woman was able to give her name and home address. Suddenly, she was not there; she was spirited away to the hospital. Despite the rapidity of the action, she made it clear something happened in the alley. I found out later what it was. At the moment it was just the detective and me.

"What are you doing here? Do you know this woman?" He looked at his note pad. "Mrs. Abrahams?"

"No. I've never seen her before this. I just happened to be here. I'm going to see *Free Willy*," I said and pointed to the movie theater just half a block away.

"*Free Willy*?" he asked. "By yourself? Aren't you a little too old for that?"

I gave him my silent look which said that there is no more to be said. He let it go.

"I may have to talk to you later. Give me your address and home phone number," the detective said.

I did with no protest.

There was nothing else for me. I considered going home, but I did not. I saw the marquee of the theatre down the street and said to myself, "Why not?"

So, in spite of the dramatic events, I saw *Free Willy*. I was so thoroughly entertained that I almost forgot everything before. I felt estranged from real life, more like a participant in the movie— helping Willy leave his bondage so that he may leap into the massive ocean where he belonged. Somehow, I felt he would never be hurt again. As I left the theater, I took a brief look down the alley the woman had escaped from and saw a door at the end. I wondered if the detective had checked that out?

Indeed, he had. I got a call from him the next day that he wanted to see me. I was eager to cooperate; I went to the station at the agreed time.

"Do know Oscar Rodriguez?" the detective asked.

No. Who is he?

"Did you see *Free Willy*?"

"Yes, of course."

He asked what the movie was about and what the plot was. I told him. I could not imagine why he wanted to check to see if I did go to the movie. I wondered, did he see *Free Willy*? Does he know the plot? Does he have kids? I think I laughed. I shouldn't have, but I did.

"You had no previous contact with Mrs. Abraham?" the detective asked.

"No, of course not."

"Well, she's very grateful to you for being there and when she recovers, she would like to reach out to you. Do you mind if I gave her your number?"

"No, of course not. I'd be happy to meet with her. Will she be all right?"

"Yes. Also, she gave me permission to tell you what happened to her. Frankly, it's a little unbelievable. Mrs. Abraham is an orthodox Jew. She had just left the Kosher Market, and she was trying to get home before sunset. You know the Jewish people put a lot of emphasis on the Sabbath and Friday night dinner. As she passed the alley, Rodriguez called to her. Normally she would ignore this kind of call from a dark alley, but he said his wife was bleeding on the bathroom floor and he needed help. He seemed genuine, at least to her he did. She put her groceries down and ran to help. Rodriguez is a crazy guy. He hates women. He didn't have a wife. At that moment—like a cat waiting for a mouse, for a meal—he saw Mrs. Abraham and wanted her. She ran to help, and he grabbed her. She saw at once there was no woman in distress and fought to get away. She managed to run toward you, and you know the rest."

"Where's Rodriguez now?"

"We've got him. This is a pretty serious predatory crime. He'll be locked up for some time. You may have to come to court to witness the injuries and the events you saw. Otherwise, I have no further questions?"

I got up to leave.

"Oh. One more question." He smiled broadly. "How did you like *Free Willy?*"

THE MILKSHAKE

E ight people in a room. It was worse than Russia. Crazy. Everyone tripping over the other. Nobody can live like this. They left Russia for this? Crazy.

Four years ago it wasn't so bad. Just the three of them. Then came Isaac, then Isaac's child, Helena, then Isaac's wife, Rumi, with the other child, Volff (when he was nine months old, he crawled around the house like a feral animal, so Heschel became Volff, and ultimately, Volffy). Of course, it was Wolf, but in the new homeland, the "W" was impossible. They were Jews after all.

I know you're counting. There's one more, right? She was born in America. Her name became Lilly because they all mispronounced Laya to make it sound like Liberty.

There was a ninth person who lived next door with another five. That was Lottie and Lottie was Volffy's aunt. Each week Lottie gave Volffy a penny.

In New York City, in 1917, there was no money. You could immigrate as a king, but you rarely got to keep your wealth. After the exchanges, the expenses, and the absence of meaningful work, you ended up struggling hand-to-mouth, or, at least, hand-to-paycheck.

After four years the family coped, but just barely. When you live like this, there are no extravagances, only necessities.

Volffy was the pride of the family—the youngest and cutest. No one knew where his white hair came from. His parents knew he was theirs. There was some speculation a Viking may have converted in the distant past and married a good Jewish girl. It was just speculation. No one could explain Volffy's hair. They simply enjoyed it.

He was a good student at the public school. He spoke better Yiddish than English, but his American was excellent. His mother depended on him to help her shop with the few new vendors who invaded the market and didn't speak the language of the old country. This was especially true when she insisted on leaving the shtetl-styled environment of 5th Street East Side, New York, to buy the slightly less expensive goods around Avenue C. Since the older Americanized Jews were business interlopers, they needed to cut a bargain, at least for a while.

He was a firm, determined, and over-confident seven year old. His sister called him stubborn. His mother countered with "serious." His friends knew that if he made up his mind, nothing would sway him. His decision might not make sense; it might even be to his disadvantage, but he would stick to his decision...no matter what.

You would think a young boy with this kind of mind-set would be a boor, but, in truth, he had a good sense of humor, and he was terrific in neighborhood stickball. He laughed at himself whenever he dug in his heels over an issue. He knew he was difficult but wondered if it mattered, all the while thinking it was funny the way people threw up their arms in frustration. Because of this agility at the local sport and the easy laughter, he had many friends and few enemies.

Like all Jews with less-than-excellent luck, his family lived in a tenement. Isaac suffered to get the job he had. Anguish, disappointments, and the frightening disappearance of the savings brought over finally led to steady employment. He was hired as a department store repairer of mannequins. He had worked as a draftsman in Russia, and he had more than the smattering of European-style education when the pogroms forced immigration. When the store heard of this, they gave him a chance, and he was a natural. Male or female, it didn't matter. He could bring back to life the model that wore the clothes his own wife couldn't afford. Unfortunately, the store paid by the piece, and there was only so many he could repair. Though he had steady work, the pay was barely above the subsistence level. Rumi often yelled at him about money. Of course, she felt the concern required for the family. The children had to be fed. His thoughts about money were indifferent at best. He worked very hard, felt a keen sense of responsibility, but knew in his heart that religion was his life.

Volffy admired his father. He saw him as a good man and wanted to be like him. He watched him lay tefillin every morning (wrapping the leather bindings around his arms) and heard, although without understanding, the prayers that thank God for leading them out of Egypt, Russia, and the pogroms. He didn't need to understand. He was inspired by the closeness felt within the family participation, the seriousness of dedication, and the respect his father showed for the ritual.

Volffy knew his parents worked hard. He saw everyone else in the building make the same lifesaving effort. Money was precious, and it was clearly the cause of fighting and yelling between his mother and father. His parents' struggle was easily compared to the bustle of the pushcarts sent against the waves of humanity clogging the streets; it was a world he felt but did not understand.

If money was precious, so was Aunt Lottie's love. Each week she gave Volffy that penny. She didn't call him Volffy though. She hated the name; she said it reminded her of the Cossacks. She had never met one, but she had heard stories. One day, she gave him a penny and waited for his hug.

During the embrace, she said, "Heschel, enjoy the penny and remember I love you."

She said it in Yiddish, so the impact would be stronger. He knew something strong had passed between them, but, at seven, he thought it was the penny.

The hug over and Aunt Lottie smiling, off he went. He ran out of the apartment, nearly tripping over his baby sister's toy. He ran down the steps, six flights of them, faster than any adult could manage and onto the streets of New York City, across the one paved block to the candy store around the corner.

Mr. Henkle saw him. He anticipated his arrival. He waved Volffy into his store. Words were unnecessary, and Mr. Henkle wasn't going to mess things up by using them. Volffy unclasped his hand and exhibited the penny for the candy store owner to take. The coin was replaced by the block of chocolate that Volffy loved. Holding the confection in his fingers, the boy stepped out of the store, leaned onto the wall next to the window filled with candies, and thought about putting the block in his mouth.

He saw the pushcarts, the people, the neighborhood kids, the sky, the weather, and the tumult. He became philosophical and reigned as the wisest sage on the street for a brief moment. He may not be Plato in his still-emerging life, but he could savor the deep sensual behavior as he plopped the wonderful creation into his mouth. Life, he felt, was a deep sensuality. Marking his existence was what his weekly anticipation was all about. Again, this week, for a penny, his being was enhanced.

This particular day, just after he had consumed his existential pleasure and reaffirmation, he walked down the street to the new luncheonette he had heard his friends talking about. He stared through the large front window and was dazzled by the bright-painted signs hung along the walls. Wire-backed chairs were placed neatly around white marble-topped tables. There was a large, wonderfully carved wooden counter extending the length of the store to one side. He dared to peek through the door and realized he could sit on one of the high stools along the counter, order something, and gaze at himself in the huge mirrored wall that extended the length of the counter.

The owner saw him and waved to him. "Come in, sit down," he said in native English.

He put his arm around Volffy's shoulders and proudly showed him the tables, chairs, the long mirror, and the magnificently fashioned counter.

"Sit." He beckoned Heschel to try the tall stool, helping him up. "Isn't this great?!" The owner beckoned.

All Volffy could say in response was yes.

Mr. Clark told Volffy to come in any time. He offered him nothing for free. It was clear that Mr. Clark was a nice man, but if Volffy wanted anything, he had to pay for it.

While Mr. Clark was showing Volffy around, a large, well-dressed woman came into the luncheonette and sat at one of the tables just feet away from where Volffy had been placed. Mr. Clark immediately went to service her and was pleased to have her order a milkshake. Volffy watched as the proprietor poured the ingredients, added the chocolate, swirled the contents vigorously with a long spoon, and finally, ceremoniously presented the completed concoction to the lady in the chic purple dress.

Volffy watched and, to his surprise, saw her consume the entire tall glass in two gulps. Time seemed to have sped up as he reasoned one of the greatest satisfactions in life disappeared faster than the velocity of the E Train. He considered how he would never drink the precious beverage in such a hasty, presumptive manner. He would only use the straw the lady had completely avoided. He would sip it slowly, maybe over an hour. He felt inwardly excited and turned his stool to Mr. Clark.

"How much does that cost?" Volffy asked, pointing shyly toward the dowager.

Six cents was the matter-of-fact reply.

Six cents. Six cents. That means six weeks. It would take six weeks of Aunt Lottie's generosity to buy the milkshake the woman drank in under three minutes. Six weeks of no chocolate. It was a sacrifice that Volffy decided then and there to make. Terrible. Six weeks. Volffy was determined.

It may surprise you to learn that Volffy thought of other things than the milkshake over the extended six weeks. Public school demanded his attention. He was determined to be a good student. His parents harped on it enough. There was also the matter of avoiding the rough Italian kids after school. Each day it was wit against wit with Volffy usually winning. This block, then that one or hold off near the corner while they passed or go through a field they usually avoided. Who could think of milkshakes during fleeing moments like that? Once home he had little time before Hebrew school. These few moments were spent talking to Aunt Lottie, the oldest person he knew. At Hebrew school, he quietly suffered the smell of Rabbi Stensky's beard. It was a long, unkempt bushy affair that all the kids snickered and made jokes about.

"Do you think that's where all the Jewish rats of New York go to hide?" they joked and laughed.

In the hour before dinner, stickball with his friends rounded out the day.

It was on Monday that he got his penny. With unabated anticipation, he cleverly cut his conversation short. With the penny in hand, he would kiss her, go across the hall to his room shared with his siblings, be sure no one was looking, and take out the pickle jar from under his clothes in his personal dresser drawer. He placed the accumulating pennies in a discarded salami delicatessen paper, wrapped them into a crumpled mess, and put the entire thing in the jar. Once the top was screwed tightly, he put it back under his clothes. He knew that if his mother or others found this, they would ignore it. He was always collecting some "silly" thing. No one would investigate further, thinking it might turn out to be a bug or worse. There was that precious experience with a still live grasshopper.

One time, it was late November; he was asked at supper what he wanted for Hanukkah.

"A milkshake, Momma," Volffy said.

Everyone laughed.

"What do you want with a milkshake, Volffy?" she said. "It's just throwing money away."

He felt embarrassed but not deterred. He decided to keep his secret to himself. His older brother, Abram, put his arm around him and told him that one day he would take him to buy a milkshake. Volffy knew this was an idle promise. Abram had no job and no wealth to squander on his desire which his mother had diminished by calling it wasteful.

Six weeks passed. Volffy had five pennies in the pickle jar. It was Monday, a fact burning vividly in his mind. He could hardly concentrate in school. "Milkshake" was a word more important than spelling "military." During arithmetic, the word appeared in his mind, and he gave the wrong answer in class. When "school" was called out, he replaced the "h" with an "n" on the blackboard. The class laughed, but he tossed it off. At recess, he kept to himself and held in his mind the image of the substantial lady in the purple dress enjoying what he was soon to have. The fact that he had no clear idea of what a chocolate milkshake tasted like did not seem to bother him. He liked chocolate candy. He assumed the drink was a delicious relative of that. He could hardly wait for school to end.

Volffy escaped the clutches of his enemies again. Hebrew school finally ended. In the middle of Rabbi Stensky's "shalom," he bolted out of the classroom. Traversing the half block to his building, he ran up the stairs to his beloved Aunt Lottie. There she sat, a Jewish Athena (the goddess of the penny) ready to grant him his wish. The goddess did not understand why he was so excited, but she did not fail to grant him his wish.

"Thank you, Aunt Lottie!"

He said this with a bellow and emphasis that caused her a bemused resignation as he finished his ritual hug. He ran to his room and took out the pickle jar. The entire six cents was now firmly clasped in his left hand as he ran down the flights of stairs toward his destination at the luncheonette.

Volffy was the only customer. He managed to climb up the stool and peer over the countertop.

He cried out with special pride: "I want a milkshake, please."

This he said in Yiddish, the language which, as long as he could remember, all important transactions occurred.

"What?" Mr. Clark asked, slightly puzzled.

Volffy realized at once that Mr. Clark's Yiddish was zero or one on the knowledge chart.

He repeated in English, "May I please have a milkshake?"

Mr. Clark smiled and said, "Good."

He began making the precious beverage without even asking for the money. Volffy, nevertheless, opened his hand, and there in the palm was six cents. The money was dropped on the counter, and the process of milkshake making continued.

Volffy couldn't sit still. He hopped off his stool and began walking around the store. He read the signs. Egg sandwiches, bagels, all manner of sweet drinks.

Mr. Clark called out, "Here's your strawberry milkshake."

Volffy turned around to return to the counter for his anticipated joy and was jolted. Strawberry?! It was a strawberry milkshake. STRAWBERRY!

Volffy was appalled, distracted, horrified, disappointed, miserable, ashamed, and completely confused. What happened next happened quickly. Volffy grabbed the glass with both hands and, being careful not to drop any of its contents, ran the half block back to his building, ignoring Mr. Clark's shocked reaction and ignoring his call: "Wait!" Not an ounce spilled up the six flights to where Volffy knew he would find Abram after his daily pursuit of a job.

"Here!" Volffy handed the glass to his brother simultaneous to this command. "Please drink, Abram. I don't like strawberry."

Abram at once took it all in and understood. He took the strawberry milkshake from his little brother. In a gesture different from that of the lady with the purple dress, he slowly drank the liquid which took six weeks to make.

While the pink liquid was disappearing into Abram, Heschel sat across the kitchen table from him with his head held in both hands. He watched with somber concentration the loss of his six weeks and six pennies. When the glass was empty, he asked Abram to keep everything a secret. Once his brother agreed, he took the glass back to the luncheonette. He handed it to Mr. Clark and did not say a word. The man was befuddled, and he could not put together what had happened. He was about to speak, but when he looked at the face of his small customer, he was silenced. Before a word could be spoken, Volffy walked out the luncheonette door.

Standing outside alone, Volffy thought of the difference between strawberry and chocolate. How was he to know all milkshakes were not the same? He took a deep breath and let it out slowly. His profound disappointment was slowly leaving him. There was nothing he could do about it anyway. He considered saving again. Is it worth the trouble? he thought. He would decide, but first, it was time for Hebrew school. Rabbi Stensky was waiting. On remembering this, Heschel left the luncheonette at once.

THE IDENTICALS

I met them for the first time in a theatre, and I never thought I would see them again. They were sitting right next to me. If I hadn't dropped my Playbill program, I would never have looked over to see two people who were exact copies of themselves. I always wondered why twins would dress exactly alike. Many don't, but these two did, even down to the leopard pin on each jacket lapel. Mine was a mere glance, but the image stuck with me. As I regained my composure and looked at the program of Albee's *Three Tall Women*, I mused at the oddity of these two. I didn't get a good look, but I was satisfied with yet another oddball New York experience.

More than a year later, I went to a book signing. Philip Roth was getting on in years. I was a fan, and so I went to Barnes and Noble to see him. I was struck by his aging, and I wondered about myself at eighty-five. It was a long line, and I hated lines. My android phone was a respite. I was reading Roth's book while I stood waiting for him to sign my hard copy. There they were, about twenty people in front, handing Roth a book. No, actually, they were simultaneously thrusting two of the same book, in the same orientation, with the same arm (I'm sure it was the right arm). I was twenty people away; that was all I could gather. Roth looked up with a wizened realization that he was experiencing the unusual. He smiled and said something. They giggled and answered. He signed the books, and they walked away. Why two books? I wondered. Couldn't they share one? This was the beginning. This was the start, even though I didn't know it at the time.

Of course, I wondered who these two were. I held no expectation I would ever find out, but months later I met them at a Manhattan party. The party moment came when Sarah was getting another drink for both of them and Susan was standing alone. I saw my opportunity, and I softly walked over to her.

"This is the third time we've met." I smiled and she returned the look.

"Really?"

"Yes. You sat next to me at *Three Tall Women,* and I saw you again at Philip Roth's book signing."

"We didn't really meet, then. You just noticed my sister and me."

"Yes, that's true. You two are noticeable. I hope you don't mind if I asked your name?"

Without hesitation, she replied, "I'm Susan. Sarah's getting us a drink."

I was beginning to feel disoriented. The idea of someone getting "us" a drink wasn't my usual translation of the situation. I let it pass and continued.

"My name is Ralph Singleton." I suddenly realized the connection. I really hadn't been thinking about it.

"That's pretty funny after meeting Sarah and me. You're joking, right?"

I laughed. "Believe it or not, I did not make the association until this moment, and I certainly would not make fun of twins by using a fake name. No. Really, the last name has always been Singleton."

"What do you do?" Susan asked in a broad smile.

"I'm an editor at Oxford Press…mainly medical books but occasionally I move laterally."

"Laterally?"

"I mean they give me a book on patient experiences with doctors or something on nutrition. Otherwise, it's mostly textbooks."

I saw a slight sigh. I was losing her quickly. Sarah came over with two drinks. I felt a wind of relief.

"This is Ralph. He's an editor at Oxford Press." There was that smile of adaptability, that charming facial expression that ends a paragraph.

"Hi." I nodded at Sarah.

The two girls were side by side. The duplication was uncanny, and it was made more otherworldly by the exact repetition of their clothes. Both were dressed alike. Both dresses had flowers of the same color, a big red carnation on a light-blue background. Their voices had the same intonation. Hair color was matched. If they were switched about quickly as in the *Which Cup Has the Marble?* game, I don't think I could have named them accurately.

Looking for a conversation gambit, I asked, "Do you two live together?"

It was meant as an innocuous question, but Susan looked at Sarah as if I had dropped a bomb.

"Why do you ask? What kind of a question is that?"

"Oh. I meant nothing by it. I'll tell you the truth. I'm struck by your peculiar twinship, and I just wondered if you also lived together or in separate apartments. I meant nothing more by it."

This wasn't true. I was thinking of calling one up for a date, and I considering how to do it. My question was deciphered somewhat correctly and she was wright to chide me. I decided immediately it would never happen.

Suddenly, Sarah turned about and abruptly said, "Nice meeting you. We've got to go. The parrot has to be fed."

She smiled broadly and grabbed Susan's hand. The two walked out. I thought that was it. They left me and the party.

I admit I was charmed and aroused. I imagined them in bed, one or the other or both. If we were undressing, would Sarah help Susan? Would both of them help me? Would one want to leave the room? How does sex work when two women are this identical? I was intrigued, but I went back to mingling, all my curiosities unsolved.

The strange discovery was that no one at the party knew them. They were noticed; I wasn't imagining them, but there was a blank expression when I asked about them. That was until I got to Gerald.

"Sarah and Susan? Yeah. Friends of mine. I've never dated them. Our relationship is more like that of siblings," Gerald said.

"Do you have their phone number or address?" I asked, "I'd like to ask one out on a date."

"Don't bother. I've never seen them separated. Anyway, it doesn't matter. Here. Let me write it down for you. They live within a few blocks from here. I wouldn't knock on the door without letting them know I'm coming though."

I took the paper from him and thanked him. I went and had a Gin and Tonic to ease my strange excitement. Standing there with my elbow on the bar and surveying the party scene, I saw nothing of interest—people trying to connect, sharing old reminiscences. It wasn't my group. I was invited because of my connection with a guy I knew at the office. There he was near Gerald. I felt that was it for the night, finished my drink, and left.

I didn't do anything. I stuck the paper with the phone number and address in my wallet but didn't act. I passed their apartment on a walk and saw nothing unusual beyond the fact that it was an expensive walk-up on the 71st between 5th and Madison. How could twins afford this? Even if the building was sublet, the location suggested big money. I felt more discouraged. I just might not be rich enough for either one or both.

At work, weeks later, a pair of twins were hired. They worked at adjoining cubicles, and they always seemed to be chatting.

"Billy-Jean and Bertha are from Arkansas," they said.

They were merely doing copy editing, so I felt no competition. I did wonder about the likelihood of two sets of mirror images coming into my life within weeks. Was I attracting this biological genomic phenomenon? No, I said to myself. It's just the spin of the roulette wheel.

Twins began popping up everywhere. There were just too many for it to be a dice game. Something odd was afoot. I'm sure others noticed. I asked Gerald what he thought of Sarah and Susan and Billy-Jean and Bertha.

"It's kind of cool," said Gerald.

"You don't think it's more than just cool?"

"No. Do you?"

Yes, I did. One afternoon, a day or so later, I saw two more sets of twins in Central Park. These were males. I felt an alarm welling up inside. I decided to act; I telephoned Susan or Sarah. Whoever answered the phone, I thought.

Frankly, I was surprised by the telephone response. She said she was Susan, but she could have been Sarah. She was very solicitous and seemed eager to have me come over. I didn't know what to make of the turn of heart. At the party, they ran away to feed the parrot. Today, Susan was willing to show me the parrot. By the way, there was no parrot. I was invited over for lunch the next day.

I had no trouble rearranging my workday. Harry, my boss, and I got along very well. He didn't care if I wanted a long lunch.

"It's your day. Enjoy it." He smiled at me in that avuncular style of his.

"Thanks," I said and went back to work.

It was a Tuesday afternoon. One of them answered the doorbell and let me in. Before that, I saw two more twins on Madison. What was going on? As I walked into the apartment, I immediately noticed the darkness. I didn't want to keep asking each twin what her name was, so I avoided using names. Neither offered her name—even though the other one joined us almost immediately, slithering into view as a copy of the first one. I thought this was somewhat inconsiderate, but I put it aside.

Why was it so dark? I wondered. Outside, the sun shone. Inside, I could hardly make out the figures of my two hosts. Fortunately, the small dining area had one big Roman window, and food was visible on the table. The girls looked attractive in their white blouses tucked into their designer jeans. They seemed eager to please, and they handed me bread, salmon on crackers, and a glass of wine. I took it all in stride and forgot my suspicions. I ate; they watched.

"You're not having anything?" I asked.

"We'll have a sandwich later. Right now, it's just wine for us."

The conversation got stuck, and I decided to plunge in.

"There have been a lot of identical twins on the streets lately. Have you noticed?" I asked.

"Yes, Ralph. That's part of the plan."

"Plan?"

"Yeah. We're taking over. Twins *über alles.*"

Now they both started giggling, and then they slapped hands together in a glee out of proportion to the joke.

"Come on. You look so worried, Ralph. We don't know why there are so many twins all of a sudden. We're just kidding you. Would you like to see the apartment?"

"Sure."

"But first, let's finish the bottle and talk awhile. Then we'll show you around."

I could swear that sometimes they talked simultaneously, but it was so exacting I couldn't be sure.

We actually drank two bottles together, and, at the end, I was feeling the alcohol.

"Come on.," the said in unison.

They took one arm each and pulled me around the apartment. I couldn't see much because it was so dark. Away from the Roman window, I felt as if I was in space with no boundaries. When I got close enough, I did appreciate the fact that there were pairs of objects scattered about. Apparently, the twins took their circumstance seriously and decorated according to their sensibility over being pairs.

Suddenly, I found myself in a large bedroom, and one of them pushed me forcibly onto the bed. At first, I thought this was going to be fun. Once the surprise passed, in less than two seconds, I realized this was the object of the invitation all along. I could have fought them off. Whatever they were, I was a man, and I had more strength than they. But my sexual fascination took over; I let Sarah climb on top of me, and she began to take off my pants. She said she was Sarah, so I knew...sort of. My penis was flailing in the air when the other one, Susan, arranged herself and sat on it. I came at once. Then Sarah did the same. To my complete surprise, I came again. I'd never been this capable.

After the second ejaculation, the girls stopped and left the room. The kissing and the intercourse were over. They clearly got what they wanted. Then, I wasn't sure what I got. I was to find out.

Within a few minutes, the pair returned.

One of them said, "Ralph, would you like a shower? The bathroom is over there."

She pointed to a corner of the large room. I could only marvel that in a mere few moments the girls had regained their composure and were fully dressed. Clearly, they now wanted me finished and out.

"Thanks," I said.

The bathroom was brightly lit with modern fixtures. The shower beckoned, so I opened the glass door and entered. Towels were waiting when I came out. I dressed and went to find my two lovers.

Back at the dining room table, coffee was waiting. Each woman extended a right hand pointing at a chair, so I sat in it. They then sat too, simultaneously as if rehearsed.

"We are not cruel, Ralph. We feel we owe you an explanation since your life is going to change radically in the next few weeks."

I suddenly became frightened.

"What do you mean?"

"We are not what we appear to be, Ralph. We appear to be humans, but we are not...exactly. I mean, we are humans, of course, but not in the way you think of them. We take the form of humans, but that is so we can reproduce ourselves as we need to be reproduced."

"What are you, then?" I meekly asked, already quite afraid of what would be the reply.

"Biomics," they answered in unison.

Relieved, I chuckled and said knowingly, "We are all biomes."

"Not in the way you're thinking." Sarah quickly replied.

I became stealthily quiet and listened.

"As you know, apparently, your body is riddled with bacteria. Every cell has one organelle, the mighty mitochondrion (the energy generator). There are bacteria throughout your gut. You cannot absorb food without them. They help fight viruses, and they populate every cell of your brain. Well, for millennia bacteria have done their yeoman duty—keeping the human body running for its lifetime, then finding another body to populate. Bacteria have always been an adjunct, an accessory. The brain, liver, gut, kidney, testicles, ovaries, muscles, skin, and so forth have been the major players. They are big organs. Each has its functions aided by bacteria. In the forties, penicillin was discovered. It wiped out the bacteria that caused illness in the human body, but it did more. Many of the natural tiny engines that survived the penicillin developed a resistance to the drug. They were also changed more fundamentally. As the new bacteria grew and spread to every cell that runs the body, they developed a communication system dependent on their numbers. Recently that number reached a critical mass and became sentient."

"Sentient? You mean aware? Bacteria became conscious?"

"Exactly. Not one neuron of your brain has consciousness, but they collectively work together to give you thought and language. Alone, your brain neurons are dullards. Together, the individual cells work to make a sentient organ. Well, bacteria are now, en masse, a consciousness, and we're taking over."

"How are you taking over?"

I began trembling with the growing realization of what Sarah and Susan (or whoever they were) were saying.

"We bugs are going to dominate your bodies and make them do what we think is best for us. No more diabetes, no more alcoholism, and no more smoking even by the remaining thirty percent of the human population.

"Does this have anything to do with all those twins I've seen populating New York?"

"Exactly! We, the biomics, discovered that pairs of humans with ourselves in domination were more effective in sustaining us than one at a time. We work in utero to split the egg of conception to make two. We could have split it again to make four, but we decided it complicated human delivery. Two at a time would do."

"How do two succeed where one might not?"

I had completely fallen apart inside. I wanted to run. But I saw the futility of it, and decided to at least understand as much as I could.

"You humans have always underestimated your own support system. We can't change your overall biology. We can only control it within each body. We realize that body sharing and communicating over time make the organism healthier. The body is never alone. This gives man salutary effects. Twins work better. Our main problem is heterogonous reproduction."

"Heterogonous reproduction?" I could not help asking.

"Yes. Your human configuration depends on a male sperm meeting a female egg. We can't make all the organs. We can't make sperms and eggs. We can affect everything once they are formed but forming them has not been discovered yet. So we need to reproduce the usual way, by having two bodies of opposite sexes unite. We did this with you today."

"I gave you sperm for a new biomic baby?"

"Yes, you did...and more."

"More?!" Now I was thoroughly spooked.

"Ralph, we have not only taken your sperm by intercourse but we have also given you developed bacteria which will take over your system in about three days or less. You will not suffer at all, at least no more than this discovery is making you suffer now with all the surprise you must be having. You are not alone. Soon we will pretty much control the human form throughout the planet. Our estimates are it will take eight years to complete the transformation. You will be a new biomic in three days, and the world will follow in a number of years."

"I'm doomed!"

"Well, you, as you know you, are doomed, but you, as a living entity, are going to enjoy a healthy and meaningful life."

"How can it be meaningful if I'm controlled by bacteria?"

"No, no, not controlled by us, replaced by us. We...you are a new earth species. You will even have memories of before, and you're not going to walk around like a zombie. Don't use the movie *The Body Snatchers* as your guide. You won't talk like robots or artificial intelligence and stare into space. We are still discovering our own 'personalities,' and it looks like we're mainly going to turn into healthier humans with some individuality of our own. You've always been our host anyway. You may not have realized until now that we've been influencing you throughout. The only change is our dominating you so you have a more stable healthy life. You humans have been irresponsible in the treatment of your bodies for centuries. There will be no more of that."

"So, you don't really fully realize what this even means for you?"

"No, we don't. We, biomics, are new creatures on this planet. We are eager to see where things go."

The talking was over. Susan and Sarah both got up and extended their right hands together. They were now impregnated by me, and they were going to have my twins, each of them. Four more biomics were going to come into the world, and they were going to be my children. Nothing about Susan and Sarah seemed artificial or odd. They had all the emotions that seemed normal. They acted for all perception like ordinary people. Clearly, I had not seen enough difference to avoid being seduced.

They walked me to the door to see me out with no concern for our continued relationship together as couples. Nothing was said about future meetings. This might be because they assumed that as I transformed into a biomic, this issue would be easily resolved. I was too stunned to say anything.

I ran to my apartment and wrote all that happened down while my body was probably beginning its transformation. I don't even know who will read this. Perhaps my new self or other biomics will find it of interest. I really don't know.

CÔTES DU RHONE

La Baraka is not that rare a name. There is a restaurant in Cuba called La Baraka. There was one in New Zealand. You would, at first, blush and then think the name is rare or unusual unless you knew its translation from the Arabic: "Good luck." When you come from a tortured country to the golden streets of America, you feel you are blessed. When you're helped by people who take a liking to you so that you build a business that supports you and your five children from scratch, you feel lucky, very lucky. Why not call your restaurant La Baraka? That was what Lucette did. She and her husband established a restaurant on Main Street in Queens and felt fortunate. La Baraka. That was what she and her charming French husband were—lucky.

José was not so lucky. Well, at first, he was. He worked hard, learning the French style of cooking. He made fish with the best of them. Once the chef, John-Luc, complimented him. The compliment was in Spanish. José had crossed the Rio Grande from Mexico but still struggled with his adoptive country's lingo. José beamed. Clearly, it was *se gusto* for him. He had a job; he was treated with

113

respect and although he was forced to live with his mother who was "legal," he had a lot of freedom to run around, drink, and enjoy the senoritas of Queens.

José was not the brightest light around. He did his work well and learned Jean-Luc's recipes, which he applied with literal exactness. His specialty besides the fish was the omelet. It's not easy to make the French omelet. It had to be buttered just right, the mixture could not be kept in the pan too long, and the turning was everything. José turned like no other Hispanic. When the time came to flip the pan, all the kitchen staff stood still watching the oblong yellow creation suspend for a moment in the air before softly landing in the pan. These were his two skills: succulent fish and the flying omelet. In everything else, he was a bumbler.

After work, he would always be the first one out the door. Certainly, the kitchen staff worked long and hard hours, but lingering over the late supper supplied by the proprietors was an implicit requirement for the spirit of the place. José gobbled his free meal left over from the day's remains and more or less ran out the door begging apologies on his way.

"Forgive me, Madam," He mumbled in Spanish. "I must go. I must."

When he did this the first time, no one cared very much. After a year of his departures—especially on Saturday nights, after a vigorous night of cooking and serving—everyone began to moan with his repeated excuses.

He was asked to stay a bit, and he tried his best to oblige. For a few months, he remained at the table with his food eaten and his leg rhythmically going up and down with nervous vigor. Everyone knew he was conforming to a demand and not agreeing that social sharing was an important part of the kitchen work atmosphere.

One night, the two owners locked the doors of La Baraka and left through the back where their car was parked. Driving out of the lot and out of view of the corner to their left, they spied José with an upturned bottle of red wine. Clearly, he had taken the bottle from the restaurant and was preparing himself for a turbulent night in the town. The car paused for the passengers to take in the scene. After José stopped drinking, he threw the half-finished bottle onto the street gutter and walked away. Jean-Luc couldn't resist. He pulled the car to the side, got out, and went to the bottle. He picked it up and looked at the label. He knew the brand well. It was a half-drunk *Côte du Rhone*.

The two owners tolerated many things, but stealing was not one of them. On Monday when José returned to work, he was confronted by both. He was shown the bottle and, in the broken Spanish that the Frenchman commanded, was told he was fired. They had the good spirit to pay him his wage for the day, but they would not let him work any further. The twenty-year-old walked out shamefaced with his head bent down. He knew he lost a good job.

Months later, José's mother came to the restaurant and introduced herself. She praised Lucette and Jean-Luc for giving her son the job. She only wished he was still alive. Lucette waited until the Hispanic mother sat down at the table and gave her order before responding. The two sat facing each another over the tablecloth when Lucette asked the question.

"What happened, Mrs. Gutteriez. Where is José now?"

Tears filled her eyes as she told the tale of her son.

"It's too simple really. He was crossing the street when cars were coming, He had done this a hundred times. I wasn't there, but if I were, I would have told him to stop being foolish. 'Wait, José,' I would have said. I said it a hundred times. He just wouldn't listen. My little boy wouldn't listen. His friend Bolero told me. He said José just missed the back of the truck passing him. He almost made it. He didn't know it was a truck carrying mirrors...big mirrors along the side. One of them stuck out. It hit my little boy in the head. He was in a coma for a week. He never woke up from the glass hitting his head. He left this life with my prayers being said over him. At least he will find God."

Lucette handed her a pink cloth napkin from the table. Her tears were flowing.

"I'm so sorry this happened. So, sorry. We all liked José. We felt very sad when he left," Lucette said.

She could not tell the poor grieving mother the whole story. She never would. This was a moment when two mothers understood each other, even if one kept a secret.

"José always talked about you and Jean-Luc: how much you helped him, how you taught him to cook. His other job paid less, but he never told me why he left here. He only said you were wonderful to him." She paused and took a deep breath. "And I must tell you how wonderful it was that you gave him so much red wine to drink, bottles and bottles he brought home. Let me thank you now for all that red wine. It was so generous of you."

Lucette did not say a word but only smiled. She was thinking over how he had not stolen one bottle but many, even cases of *Côte du Rhone*. How could they have missed the loss? He must have been doing it for months.

Instead of these thoughts, she only said, "I'm so glad you enjoyed the wine. Let me get you another bottle."

She quickly went to her wine rack, pulled out a *Côte du Rhone*, and presented it to Mrs. Gutteriez.

The poor woman held the bottle to her breast as if it were José himself.

"Also, Mrs. Gutteriez, the lunch is on us in the memory of your son."

La Baraka.

THE MAN WHO WANTED TO PLAY THE CELLO

S am was forty, and he loved his wife, Jenny. After twenty-two years of marriage, he decided to take up the cello. Jenny was very encouraging.

"You need a hobby," she said. "The Sunday Times is not enough. You need more."

Sam bought a cheap cello and began to practice. The kids laughed because he sounded awful. Jenny smiled at the pleasure of seeing her husband enjoy himself. It's a healthy thing, she thought. They were a little surprised when he called a teacher and began to take lessons. The weekend was punctuated by Sam's practicing. The squeaks and twangs were tolerated with smiles and horizontally shaking heads. He felt good when he realized the family was behind him 100 percent.

Attitudes began to change as Sam got more involved. The altered atmosphere developed insidiously. He began to love the cello. On returning from work, he would begin by being especially nice to hide the fact that he could hardly wait to practice his cello.

Nobody was fooled. Even during the first week, his disappearance into the basement was felt as a preference for the cello over everyone at the dinner table.

The second week was a different matter. Jenny started. She made a special meal, duck *à l'orange*, and plied him with some red wine and some gentle, nudging questions.

"Sam, you're practicing two hours a night. It's a little much don't you think? Could you cut it to one? The kids are feeling neglected. Olive is only five, you know. She wants more of her daddy."

All of this flew over his head. He did not tune in to Jenny's concern. Still, he agreed to play only an hour and not on the night of his lesson. He was sorry this new hobby was so bothersome. He did not see the storm coming.

By the third week, the cello, in Jenny's mind, had become another woman. She could not stand seeing him hug the instrument. She looked at her own image in the mirror and considered her aging physique. Perhaps she should be more coquettish? If they had sex more frequently, maybe the cello would be less alluring?

The two kids began to have fights while Sam was practicing, forcing him to come up to stop them. It never occurred to him the fighting was a devious method to force him to leave his beloved instrument. Jenny had her own temper tantrum by the fourth week. Sam listened. He said he was sorry. He didn't mean to cause such disruption. He was not going to stop, but he would try to be more considerate—less obsessed nightly by his growing compulsion.

That discussion calmed the house for a few days. Sam continued to play. It seemed his practice times took longer and longer. The kids were having problems in school. Sam seemed oblivious of the effect he was having.

After dinner on the Tuesday of the fifth week, Sam left the table before Jenny was through eating.

"Damn you!" she screamed. "You do nothing around here. You never help around the house. How dare you leave me with the kids before we've finished eating? All you think about is that damned cello."

"Since you've been stroking it," she said with dripping feminine sarcasm, "the marriage has become a sham. You're not a husband. You're a 'cello man.'" She liked that one.

She continued: "Olive's teacher told me she has begun biting her nails, and she seems distracted in class. I got a note from Phillip's teacher that he has stopped handing in his homework. While you're fiddling, everything's falling apart."

"I'm not fiddling," he shouted back. "I'm playing the cello!"

Her rage increased.

Fired by the interpretation that he cared little for his family and could only respond to the topic of his precious instrument, she retorted, "As far as I'm concerned, it's a fiddle and you're ridiculous. This hobby has turned in an unintended direction. You're obsessed. You've got to stop. You've got to!

Sam felt sudden guilt. She began to cry, and he tried to put his arm around her to comfort her. She shrugged him off.

"Just tell me you'll stop. That's all I want to hear," Jenny said.

Sam lowered his head. There was a long silence.

He looked up with doleful eyes: "I can't, Jenny. I don't why it means so much to me. It's not that I don't care about you and the kids...not at all. I will try hard to get more involved with the kids. I don't like what you said about their school. I'll play in the basement only after they've gone to bed, but I can't give up the cello."

Jenny stared at him with a historic scowl. She turned, threw the dish towel on the floor, and ran to their bedroom, slamming the door in her wake.

Sam made half-hearted attempts to keep his promise, but Jenny and the kids felt his alienation. She tried to keep a lid on things, not to make a scene. Slowly she put on weight. Sam noticed. He always enjoyed her good looks, and he saw she was caring about herself less and less. It bothered him, but he discovered he couldn't talk about it. Every time he did, she would immediately cry and curse the cello. Sam became silent.

As Sam got better at playing, the marriage got worse. Jenny took the kids to live with her mother. His mother-in-law was a bad influence on the kids. She was either overly critical or too free with the candy. Sam talked Jenny into coming home while he agreed to move to an apartment in New York, an hour from the Long Island home.

In the beginning, he missed his family. He changed and then substituted his cello for the family feeling. He called weekly, but Jenny refused to talk to him. He paid for everything. His accounting job was the only thing competing with the cello now. He played constantly and even begrudged sleep.

The cello playing was improving. His teacher wanted him to play with a pianist, but Sam was too shy, thinking his passages weren't smooth enough. He struggled with Bach. He thought about passages throughout the day, and it was affecting his usual accuracy and diligence at his accounting firm. He took days off from work to practice. It was on such a day that he heard a knock on his door. It was a messenger handing him an envelope. He was so preoccupied that he took it from the guy and did not think to give a tip. He opened the envelope to find a carefully worded termination of employment from his boss, who always praised his work. There was money in the bank. His boss was a caring man; he provided a nice termination package.

Another year passed, and Sam had to write Jenny about stopping the checks. He explained that he was going on disability. He found a clinical psychiatrist who would certify he was emotionally disabled. Certainly, he would send all he could, but maybe Jenny should look for work. His new address would be one of those welfare apartments with broken elevators. "Now I climb up four flights with my cello." Jenny cried when she read this.

Sam could not pay his first teacher, so he hired a desperate Juilliard student who cost him much less. Lessons were now every other week. He was practicing four or five hours a day. He thought the slow movement of the Bach suites sounded pretty good. There were some complaints in his apartment building that he disturbed the children's sleep during the day. He then thought maybe he could play outside.

He found a space outside the Hallmark card store on 55th and 5th Avenue. He had been pushed out of another spot where a wind quartet was already in place. He began to supplement his welfare income; he was always surprised anyone would drop a dollar in his hat for a few moments of amateur music. Fortunately, no one stayed very long to discover that he was playing the same part of the Bach suite over and over.

Jenny divorced Sam. He never returned to his job. Jenny and the family adjusted. She began to date, but she always hoped someday Sam would return to his senses. The kids got better in school and only talked about their father when they planned to see him. They knew he was in front of the Hallmark card store every night except on Sunday, but they rarely went to see him play there.

On one occasion they begged their mother to drive them to see Sam in the city. She parked the car two blocks away and let the kids out. As they made their way toward their father, Jenny sat silently behind the wheel of the car asking herself how a crazy situation like this one could ever happen to her. She couldn't bring herself to see Sam on his spot. It was just too unsettling. The kids finally stood in front of their father while their mother watched from the distance.

Sam looked up at them and smiled but never stopped playing his Bach slow movement of the same suite. After five or ten minutes of this, the kids made a tender gesture of goodbye. He acknowledged them with a sweet nod of his head. They walked back to the car while Jenny watched.

The story ends here.

Sam is still playing; the cello is all that has meaning to him. He is separated from everyone. The family is doing all right. Jenny, Olive, and Phillip are not as happy as Sam. They always feel something is missing. Whenever they think of Sam, they are consoled by the idea that he really did learn to play the cello. They all agree that, to them, he played pretty well.

MYXOMYCETES PLASMODIUM

D r. Cohen was the world's leading expert on that weird amoeba fungus, and he had just delivered and set up one of the world's earliest electron microscope. For a tiny school like Oglethorpe, this was no small matter.

"Do you want to see it?" Dr. Cohen asked. "It's in the basement. A lot of money."

"Yeah." The sophomore nodded in eager agreement.

He couldn't believe it was true. He had read about it in the 1958 issue of the Scientific American magazine. Here it was in the basement of his dormitory. This wasn't such a backward school. He was glad he'd accepted the scholarship. He was glad he'd met Dr. Cohen, the author of the subject on myxomycetes plasmodium in the Encyclopedia Britannica. The title of his encyclopedia article was *Slime Molds*. He was excited and reassured that he was at a school on the cutting edge of science. This was the real thing.

He and Julius followed Dr. Cohen from the classroom and went downstairs. The instrument had a room of its own. It wasn't a big room. The room was a little dusty. The entire magnificent modern invention sat on a desk.

"Isn't it dark?" He asked the chubby slightly balled Jewish professor of biology.

"You need it dark to work. The screen is dimly lit. It's electrons that provide the light."

The two sophomores stood in rapt gaze at the ultramodern image maker.

"Do both of you know what a myxomycetes plasmodium is?" Dr. Cohen asked.

Both shook their heads from side to side.

Dr. Cohen said, "It's weird. You'd find it spread out in a yellowish mass under a log in the woods. That's its slime phase. If you put it on a petri dish and watch it a few days, it will transform into stalks. Here let me show you."

Dr. Cohen flicked a switch, and the contrivance began to hum. He seemed to know what he was doing. He then placed a slide inside a unit beneath what must have been a tubular microscope. This tube conduced electrons against the matter on the slide.

"Okay, let's put the mycetes on the viewing screen," said Dr. Cohen.

There on the black and white image was a set of spores on stalks sticking into the microscopic void.

"You'd think that is the end of it, but this little creature has more tricks than you would expect," said Dr. Cohen.

Dr. Cohen was getting excited. He took that slide out and put in another. The screen then showed an amoeba. It wasn't easy to see, but the professor said that this creature moved.

"It's still the mycetes transformed into a moving animal, not a plant." He smiled. "So what's a plant and what's an animal? This creature goes back and forth. If the electron microscope didn't fry it into no motion, you could have seen it in all its phases: amoebic, then plasmodium mass, then stalks forming, then sporulation and the spreading of the new seeds, and back to amoeba again. It's fantastic."

The students were amazed. For the rest of their lives, they would never forget this moment when the great Dr. Cohen taught them about the nether world of animal and plant.

Weeks later, the two students met on the quadrangle between the gothic-styled buildings of the Oglethorpe campus.

"Hi, Julius. How's it going?" the sophomore asked.

Julius looked glum-faced. "I didn't get in."

The sophomore knew exactly what he meant. "What happened, Julius?"

"It was Cohen."

"Really, what did Cohen do?"

"He saw me looking over on someone's labs. He decided then and there I was no material for medical school. Without saying a word to me, he wrote a letter to the medical school and told them what happened. The school actually sent me a copy of the letter. It said I did not have the character to be a doctor. I'm screwed."

"Did you talk to Cohen?"

"Yeah. He was rigid. He was absolute. He said being a doctor was too high a calling to allow someone who cheats, even once, into the profession. He sounded like a religious fundamentalist to me. I asked him why he didn't talk to me, help me through one indiscretion. He said he didn't need to talk to me. I made my bed, and I will lie in it forever. You know what's funny about this?"

"What?"

"I wasn't even cheating. I looked over in the direction of William but couldn't even see his paper. I never got a chance to say this to Dr. Cohen. It was hopeless."

"That's terrible Julius. It's so unfair."

"Well, it's done. I always wanted to go into biochemistry anyway. Dr. Cohen said he would recommend me for a graduate school position in biochemistry, just not medical school. I don't know why a cheater can be a biochemist but not a doctor? Weird."

"It is weird. Just like myxomycetes plasmodium."

THE BICYCLIST

We could hardly see the road as we made our way to the air base five miles from Taichung. The car lights were more visible than the ruts and holes that suddenly emerged in its path. Pavement was a thing of the future. It was only 1968. Rural Taiwan was a deserted terrain of what was still a third world country.

We were not late, Lisa and I. It was a dance with a buffet, not a seated dinner. I was a mere captain; I was just another doctor assigned to the Air Force base from the United States. I would not be noticed if I arrived late to the officer's reception—especially if it was because I drove slowly in this stygian darkness with nothing to guide me but the light beams on the muddy road ahead.

"Thirty kilometers an hour. Does that seem too fast?" I bragged to my companion.

"It's so dark; maybe you should go slower." Her sarcasm betrayed her inability to convert to miles per hour, and I took exception.

"I'm only going about eighteen miles an hour, Lisa. Give me a break."

My wife of five years usually became silent at my aggression, however mild. For a long stretch, the only sounds that we heard were the rattling shocks of the car, as an unanticipated hole had sent us bouncing into the night air. It was a relief to have come down safely.

Suddenly, someone emerged in front of our car. My lights hit him on his bicycle before I did. I applied the brakes but heard the crash of my vehicle hitting metal. Strangely I did not hear him cry out.

Lisa did it for him: "Oh my God! Is he dead? Oh, terrible. Terrible."

I thought to leave the lights on as I shut the engine and got out of the car. I had the passing thought this might have been staged to rob us, but there he was lying beneath his own wheels. He was a common man, one like so many other Taiwanese I might have hit.

He looked at me with suffering eyes. His pain from life seemed to me as momentous as my injuring him. I reminded myself I was a doctor and went to check his pulse. He spoke no English and made a gesture that I should back away from him. He waved his hand from side to side suggesting he was not seriously hurt.

"Name?" He asked.

His English consisted of just that. From the darkness, other people emerged.

A sensible-sounding male voice intervened: "I speak English. He wants your name and phone number to call. Can you give him that? We take him to the hospital. Okay?"

I went to the car and rummaged in the glove compartment for a piece of paper. I wrote my military name, my position, and my phone number and then tried to give it to my victim. Before I could hand over my information, the man who came from the darkness grabbed it from my hand.

He said, "I give it to him. He will go to hospital. He call tomorrow. Okay?"

Is it okay? What else am I to do on this dark road? I asked. "Will he be safe without me? Maybe I should take him to the hospital. The car is faster?" I felt the darkened face looking at me.

"No, no. This bad road. Two roads meet. This happen many times. We know what to do. You go. He call maybe tomorrow, maybe next day."

During all this, the bicyclist was sitting in the mud beside his bike, showing no sign of significant suffering. I was clearly out of my element, and I was being asked to beat a hasty retreat. I felt I could do little more.

I got back into the car and held Lisa's trembling hands for a moment of reassurance.

"I guess we'll go on. He says he's all right. I'm not sure where the hospital is or what we'll be able to do there. Clearly, he is not in an emergency. Frankly, Lisa, the whole thing makes me very uncomfortable. I feel I should see this through, but the guy who took my information seemed as if he'd done this before. I don't want to be the 'ugly American,' but I think we should just go."

Then it occurred to me. "Wait!"

I hurriedly got out of the car and said into the dark crowd of vague figures: "What is your name?"

I don't know who answered but I heard an unintelligible utterance and the clearly announced "Chang."

As I returned to the car, I called out, "All right, Mr. Chang. I hope you will be fine, and I look forward to helping you more. Get in touch with me, please."

I used all the earnestness at my disposal. I was trying to cover my guilt as well as I could. This was hard to do as I rode off to my reception in my 1968 red Datsun.

⚊⧼⊢⊣⧽⚊

We were quite shaken. This was the only person I had ever hurt for any reason. I wasn't sure I was guilty of poor judgment or poor driving because I convinced myself that I was being very careful. Also, Mr. Chang could see me, but I could not see him. How did he come to be crossing the road just as I came by? I shared these thoughts with my fellow officers.

Eddie, in particular, had a jaded view of the whole affair: "These things happen here all the time. They set up a minor accident and make a few bucks. I wouldn't worry about it. Just play along."

I didn't know what to make of Eddie's offering, and I mentally swerved between using it to shake off my sense of committing a crime and remorse for leaving the scene and not adequately helping a fellow human being.

The next day I heard nothing. By the third day, I began to believe the entire affair had been lost in the midst of misidentification and poor information. Then I got the note. The base adjutant wanted to see me.

"Sit down, Captain," he said.

I did.

He continued: "Do you know anything about an accident involving you in a vehicle, driving on the road to the air base, and a Mr. Chang riding a bicycle two nights ago?"

I answered, "I do."

"Well, we don't want these things getting out of hand. So, you have to make restitution."

I felt defensive, while my guilt was sequestered.

"You know, I was driving eighteen miles an hour and my headlights were clearly visible, but Mr. Chang suddenly darted out in front of me. I think he's the responsible party here!" I was instantly ashamed of my outburst. "Sorry. I'm very bothered by the whole thing."

"You need to appreciate, Captain, that we've had a number of these incidents. Fighting these people gets us into an entangling mess. It could drag on and even affect your discharge schedule. The best thing is to give restitution and show your remorse."

"Restitution and remorse?"

I quickly calmed down and decided a more cooperative manner was more useful. Besides, the adjutant was treating me well, and he really only wanted to get this behind us: me and the Air Force.

"Restitution comes to a hundred dollars. Remorse means it's best you visit him at the hospital and make a gesture, showing sadness and regret over the entire matter."

<--<|>-->

Lisa didn't want to come. The adjutant told me where the hospital was and how to get there. Surprisingly the dilapidated building had an information desk.

"Mr., Chang?" I requested.

The man did not say a word, but he wrote down "3D" on a piece of paper. I went up the three flights before me and found 3D. I hesitated. I walked in.

There before me was my victim in a rumpled bed. Here I was in uniform. The other eight or nine men, women, and children were sitting on the floor. When I entered, everyone stood up. A woman who might have been Mr. Chang's wife came and clasped my hand with a grateful 172 squeeze. I bowed and gestured sadness. I went up to the man I presumed was Mr. Chang and wiped his brow with a cloth I saw next to his bed. He pointed at his arm, which was in a cast. I pointed at his arm in acknowledgment. There were orange peels on the floor amid bowls of food. These were in disarray, and hygiene was clearly poor. The clothes worn by those in attendance were those of farmers and field workers. The feeling in the room—the emotional atmosphere that I don't think I misinterpreted—was that of thankfulness to me. I walked over to Mr. Chang and put a hundred dollars in his other hand. He bowed his head in gratitude. His family and I were in a tacit agreement of understanding and forgiveness. Mr. Chang had suffered to help them, and I had gone along as if everything was as it was presented to be. I put my hand over my heart to show affection and concern. Everyone bowed to me. I made a small bow in return and left the room.

I had shown restitution and remorse, and Mr. Chang, his family, and his entourage had shown gratitude. Nothing more was ever heard about the matter. I finished my tour of duty months later. No papers were signed regarding Mr. Chang. No further demands were made.

THE TRIAL OF CAIN

T he judge entered the room.
    "Hear ye! Hear ye! The honorable Judge Tobias Ismael is in
the court. All rise!" the courtroom clerk announced.

The case had been the talk of the nation. The courtroom was
packed. The controversy surrounding this murder had stirred
enmity between family members, frustration between friends, and
multiple fights on the streets.

The court, where this final determination of guilt or innocence was to take place, was beautiful. The building was old, and
it had excessive decoration on its pillars and pediments. The room
inside was wood-paneled, and it possessed carvings four dedicated
German craftsmen proudly put in place. Above the dais where the
judge sat, the wall exhibited a large figure—carved with flowing,
undulating tresses, giving the impression of an observing deity.
The man represented was known not as a mythic figure but as
Pearl Last. This was a fact demonstrated by the carefully inscribed
name to the left of the face. Mr. Last clearly wanted the world to
know his work, but he was not expecting that the configuration
itself would come to possess his identity. Nevertheless, the staring

visage with its solemn lip turned downward and beady eyes allow-ing no one in the court to feel relaxed had the effect of God's pres-ence. The message of the carving was that this was a serious place of serious business, and all were witness to a transported human power. The judge and the menacing face of Pearl Last's transfigu-ration dominated everything, and they were hard to shake aside.

At this point in the trial, all of the prosecution witnesses but one had been seen. A Mr. Abrad was on the stand as the last. Once the judge was seated and all the lawyers were in place, the ques-tioning continued. He claimed he had seen the reported conversa-tion which spirited the accused, Cain, to commit the crime. Mr. Abrad did not see to whom the accused was speaking.

"Cain was talking to a voice," Mr. Abrad said.

"A voice?" the prosecutor asked uncertainly.

"Yes, it was a voice in a whirlwind."

"Who was this voice you heard?"

"I don't really know."

"Did the accused give it a name?"

"Yes."

"What name was that?"

"He called him God."

Suddenly, there was a good deal of rustling in the court seats, but no one snickered or cried out. The trial had proceeded so far with this kind of material. The audience had become used to the fantastic situation. The judge had called either lawyer on very few points of law. It seemed the idea of God talking to the accused had nothing illegal about it and demanded no explanation. One either accepted the witness's testimony or not.

In this instance, the witness agreed completely with the asser-tion of the accused, as reported by the local newspaper. His con-tention was the very argument his lawyer planned on using to sup-port the defense. That is, God made him commit the crime.

It was still early in the morning. The judge called a recess to allow the attorneys prepare their final arguments. When they returned and the court was called again to be quiet, the defense counsel asked for Cain to come to the witness stand.

"Please state your name before the court," said the defense counsel.

"My name is Cain."

"Do you have a first name?"

"That is my first name."

"Do you have a last name?"

"That is my last name."

It was clear that the defense was trying to establish Cain's significance as being beyond that of ordinary men. By suggesting Cain lived on a different plane than the average person, an element of mystery was introduced into the case. Everyone had grown used to this aspect of the trial. The reaction to the interchange was a continuation of this grand silence that persisted throughout the proceedings.

Cain's lawyer was Jewish. He had decided earlier in the proceedings to de-emphasize this fact. Since Cain's roots were in the Jewish tradition, the jury might have lumped the two men together in their thinking. Whatever feeling of prejudice in them would have been encouraged. So Mr. Ablestein took on the form of a New England man of the bar. He was dressed in a very conservative suit, with a vest to match. The gray tweed mitigated against his ethnic background. There was a rumor among the press that he had once sported a beard and had expressly shaved it for this case. Since there was no documentation concerning whether his beard was removed or when it was, nothing could have been definitively concluded.

Ablestein stood erect and spoke precisely and decidedly to his client: "Please tell the jury, in your own words, what transpired on the day of the alleged crime."

This was a dangerous gambit, and Ablestein was quite aware of what he was chancing. Though Cain had originally pled "not guilty" over the killing of his brother, it was clear to all that he had indeed killed him. Ablestein wanted to establish that his crime had extenuating circumstances so powerful that the killing was, in fact, not Cain's doing. This was a tricky subtlety. The door was open. There was no closing it now.

"Do you want the events directly connecting to my brother's death or do you want the entire day's events?" Cain asked.

Cain was completely composed. Perhaps too much so for the jury's liking, Ablestein thought. Yet this composure was better than any dramatic gestures or attempts to convince.

"Begin with the early morning and continue until your brother's death," said Abelstein.

"I awoke about four o'clock. I remember the day so well. The sun was high in the sky, even at that hour. It was early summer. The heat was tremendous but still tolerable. The blue sky had that deep early morning cobalt color, a color we desert people love. I was in an especially good mood. This was the day my father and mother told Abel and me to give to God the fruits of our labors."

"Tell the jury about the gifts."

Ablestein bent slightly toward his client as he spoke loudly and distinctly. The jury did not miss the idea that the composed lawyer felt this question to be especially important.

"My parents told me about God's wish, but I also believed I came upon the idea in a dream. God was forever checking on our family. He had been disappointed since my parents forced him to send them out from paradise."

He paused for effect, assuming everyone knew to what he referred. Ablestein didn't stop him from explaining, so he continued.

"Despite my parents' mistakes, God said he blessed them, and he would make their fields fertile and their sheep fecund. I didn't know about this original promise. My parents told me about it."

He paused again, as if musing on his childhood. Altogether he was making a good impression on the jury.

Cain continued, "The fact is the food was bountiful, and our table was always filled from corner to corner. We wanted for nothing."

"Yes. So, everyone—you, Abel, Adam, and Eve—knew that you owed your daily comforts to the Lord?" Ablestein was going for effect again.

"We knew this in our souls, but God wanted an indication of the obvious. He wanted us to show he was appreciated, and his goodness should be embraced with an adoration knowing no bounds. This was his need, especially after the sins of my parents in Eden."

"Did God say all this to you?" Ablestein interrupted.

Suddenly, the prosecuting attorney stood. His rotund frame insisted on immediate attention.

He cried out: "I object, Your Honor. The existence of this God has not been established. The witness is attempting to seduce the court with his fantasy. Must we listen to this poor farmer's field make-believe?"

"Your Honor!" Ablestein literally jumped toward the bench to reply. "The story is crucial to my client's defense. It is irrelevant at this juncture whether or not God is a reality—though I believe a review of this court's record of this trial will show that a good case has been made for it. What is at stake here is my client's version of what happened. I merely want him to be allowed to tell it as he saw it."

"Objection overruled. The witness has a right to tell the story as he sees it. Continue," the judge instructed.

Ablestein saw the momentum had been lost. He tried to bring back the mood by repeating, "Did God say he wanted an indication of the family's appreciation of his care?"

"In my dream, God spoke to me. My father, Adam, also said he had spoken to God. I remember my father's exact words: 'Bring me your offering from the fruits of your labor.'"

"Those were God's words, not your father's, right?"

"Yes. I think I'm quoting God through my father here."

"Go on, Cain. So this morning in question you planned to obey?" Ablestein urged.

"Of course. Yes. My fields had done very well. I had worked hard. The rains and sunshine were doing their job and were well-balanced in their effects. I was satisfied and proud of what had been produced. I looked forward to reaping the best part of my field and giving it bountifully and lovingly to God. There was no anxiety, no rancor, and my heart was at peace. I was a happy man."

The poor fellow put his head in his hands and began to cry. Ablestein did not lose sight of this opportunity. He stood and looked plaintively at the jury with his hand on his hip. The crying continued for a full minute. The court was forced to listen in silence. Then the lawyer turned back toward his client and asked him if he could continue.

The gentle nudge from his defense attorney bred results, and Cain responded. He lifted his head from his hands and wiped his eyes, showing he had been unquestionably overwrought. His departure from his story with overwhelming emotion had not been staged. This was a man in genuine despair. The jury could see.

"I reaped the best part of my fields and went to give all I gathered to God. My cart was filled with wheat, vegetables, rye, and marvelous fruits from the trees—I picked them the moment just before falling; they were filled with the juices of exquisite flavor fit for a god. I felt sure my obedience would be rewarded or, at least, appreciated for the devotion I wanted to show. I knew, I felt, I believed I was giving God the best of my labors."

He looked up at the filled room and continued: "Pulling my cart toward the place where I would pass onto God my offerings was hard work. There was a steep incline upward, and it was hard going. I had to do all the work by hand; the help of an ox was not part of our bounty. Because the steep hill and terrain held me to a slow pace, my brother, Abel, got to the top of the hill first. I saw him ahead of me just as I reached the crest."

Ablestein interrupted, "Tell the court what else you saw at the top of the hill?

"As the edge dropped away, I looked up and saw the sunlit day disappear. In its place was a swirling cloud, its darkness obliterating the sun. The cloud was thick, and its winds drove the sands of the earth about, making it uneasy to see at all without wiping one's eyes repeatedly."

"Yet I saw Abel with a very fine young firstling from his flock. I heard him say prayers to God. I noted to myself to say the same prayers and add my own heartfelt feelings to show my gift was as well-meant as Abel's. I stood on the side with my cart filled with my precious produce. I saw Abel stab his cultivated lamb, drawing blood from his neck. He then held high his sacrifice before the grayness of swirling space above us. The dead lamb miraculously disappeared into the firmament. There was no trace of blood on the ground. Abel's knife was clean as if it had never been used. My brother was awestruck. So was I."

The lawyer, the court, and the jury were awestruck as well.

"Was there a sound? Did God speak to Abel?"

Ablestein seemed subdued. It was impossible for anyone not to be captivated by Cain's tale. The prosecutor was silent and sullen.

"Yes, God spoke. He told Abel he was very pleased with the sacrifice. He said that Abel showed his respect, and in return, he would receive God's loving benefice. My brother beamed with delight."

"Did you see the form of God? Was there a figure, a shape of a person, a man, anything?" The lawyer whispered these words so that the jury could hardly hear him.

"No, no. There was no shape, only the deep, resonating sound of a voice from above. There was nothing more. The cloud, the grayness, the swirls of sand, and that all-embracing authoritarian voice."

"Then it was your turn?"

"Yes."

"Was Abel there for your donation? Did he watch as you did for him?"

"I believe he did. I am not sure. I saw another figure on another hill some distance away. I believe that was Mr. Abrad though; I couldn't be sure of that either."

"Go on."

"Well, I pulled my cart to the spot where Abel had stood. I looked upward into the cloud. I didn't know where else to look. I said all the prayers Abel had said. I said them all, every one of them. I am sure I left not a word out."

Cain became animated. He was clearly agitated, and anger emerged from his countenance.

Cain continued: "Then I was inspired. I added obeisance in words of my own. I became enthusiastic but was completely sincere. I was completely honest with God!"

Cain made a fist. He lifted his arm upward into the court air. His anger, his bitterness was there for all to see.

His lawyer tried to prevent him from an outburst. He interrupted with calming words: "Cain, we know that the entire matter has been an ordeal for you. It is important that you contain yourself, so the jury can get the entire story. Please continue. You were saying that you gave your sincere and enthusiastic prayers. What happened next?"

The words were successful, the intervention was effective. Cain gathered his composure.

"I finished my prayers and stood to look around me. Strangely, the swirling sands had abated. The gray cloud seemed lower. I felt anticipation, uncertainty, but at ease with my devotion to God. I knew what I had to do. I pushed the cart with my gifts to a point immediately beneath the cloud now a mere ten feet off the ground."

"And then?" Ablestein nudged gently.

"And then the cloud gently caressed the cart and lifted it into the void without a single fruit falling to the earth."

"Are you suggesting it was another miracle, like the miracle that you witnessed happening with Abel?"

"I am."

"You are saying, then"—Ablestein turned toward the jury with a look of humility and abjectness, making it impossible not to be transported to a moment of special transcendent sensibility—"that you and Abel shared, for a brief moment, the awesomeness (the frightening power) of a being whose existence goes beyond anything we earthly humans can imagine?"

"There is no force like God's force. There is no power like God's power. God is the black hole, the antigravity, the greatest magnificence of any galaxy. God is the supernova, the exploding nebula, the connecting fiber for all things. Even 'is' becomes too humble a concept to describe the swirl of penetrating presence I felt on that hill that day. Yes, for a short time, I felt it. I felt it as did my mother and father as they were sent from paradise. I felt what my poor dead brother felt." He began to sob again. "How am I to redeem myself for what I have done?!"

The entire court gasped. The guilt had been admitted in open court. Was the case lost? The judge called both attorneys before the bench.

Whispering, the judge said, "Ablestein, is your client making a confession in open court?"

Ablestein decisively uttered in reply, "No, Your Honor. He is quite distraught. Even Cain cannot pronounce on his own guilt. I have his permission to tell you he maintains his plea of not guilty. The question before the court, Your Honor, is not whether Cain killed Abel. We know that he did. The question is whether he is *guilty* of killing Abel, Your Honor." Ablestein emphatically pronounced the word "guilty" with the blow of his verbal hammer.

"I deeply believe he is not guilty, and I wish to demonstrate this to you and the jury."

At this point, the prosecutor, Mr. Goncrist, a man who had once practiced as a Congregationalist minister, mumbled about his view that the entire proceeding was a dubious enterprise. He, however, did not press the point.

The judge scowled at him, virtually arresting any further comment, and said, "Very well, Ablestein, proceed. Be alert to the fact, however, that you are walking a thin line. There is no precedent for allowing murder to be based on hallucinations without simultaneously raising the mental illness defense which you have not done. You must establish that what occurred with Cain was due to more than a mere psychotic belief."

"Yes, Your Honor."

The two lawyers returned to their respective places. Ablestein looked at the jury, bowed slightly, and then looked at Cain and asked, "Are you all right?"

"Yes, thank you."

"Cain, please tell the court what happened next."

"God took what I had offered and then said he was displeased. I was thunderstruck. I was terrified. My first thought was whether or not he would kill me on the spot. Once I realized he was not going to do that, I then considered why my efforts were unsatisfactory. I cried into the gray swirl of opacity above me: 'Why, oh Lord, art though displeased with me?' There was no answer. Painful silence passed. My anxiety and perplexity increased. I was frozen before the emptiness and silence. It seemed as if only God and myself were present, even though I know, or thought I knew, that Abel was nearby. Finally, the voice spoke out in the deep tones of an earth rumble: 'You have not brought offerings from the fruits of your labor!' I had absolutely no idea what he meant. Had I not picked the best fruits from the trees? Had I not reaped the first of my grown fields and discarded all that was not fit? Had I not loaded the cart with my own hands and pushed it up this hill under my own labor? What else did God want? Did he want all my fields? If so, he could have all. Abel gave a single lamb, and God was pleased. My confusion crept through my desert skin, and my spirits sank into darkness. There were no answers to the questions that I spoke not only to myself but also to the gray mass above me. I fell to the ground, and the cloud disappeared. Torment rose in me. I thought, Why did Abel please God, and I did not? Why did he get a 'yes' and I a 'no'? Where is the order and fairness in this universe? Now I am not to be blessed by God. My fields will lie fallow. My fruits will not appear for harvesting. I am lost."

"Was this terrible, life-threatening, and irreversible for you? Was there no way out? Had God spoken?" Abelstein asked.

"Yes. Then Abel approached. I did not look at him at first. I was immersed, like Job, in my abject despair. I felt his presence, and from my position, kneeling upon the earth, I looked up at him. There he was. His face was possessed by his serene smile. He was smiling because of his encounter with the Lord. If that smile had not been there...maybe nothing would have happened. I don't really know. To me, at that moment, Abel's smile had been placed on his lips by God. It was an expression that tormented me. It was a statement that, for the reason of chance or God's arbitrary whim, I had been 'chosen' not to have the feeling now painfully visible on my brother's face. I was the discounted one. I knew, suddenly, in a flash of insight that God had decided one of us was to have and the other was not to. I was to be the loser; it could have been Abel who was chosen, but it was not. It was me. My doubts accumulated. I tried to understand. Was this happening because Abel had a small lamb to carry, making him reach the top of the hill first, while I had a heavy cart? Then Abel spoke to me in his serenity: 'I am sad for you, brother. Be at peace. I am sure God knows you, and he will bless you.'

"With these words, I jumped from my kneeling position and, in one surprising motion, brought out my field knife and killed him. I killed Abel and denied God. It was a swift act born of no decision. It was my act of passion against God. I do not think I wanted to kill my brother. I wanted to avenge an unjust God. Mine was an act born of futility. Had God not been displeased with me? Was there anything I could do to please God? Had I not lost all? Why inhibit myself? Why check my passions? I thought none of these at the moment of Abel's death. I am sure it was all rushing through my brain like a cataract accepted only by the rocks below."

There was complete silence; all were stunned, hushed. The story was well-known from the newspapers, but Cain's soul could not be captured in those articles. His tone was resignation; his delivery was passionless. The uninhibited thrust of the knife was accompanied, in its reporting, with a stoic staring. Cain had just told of the killing of his brother with the delivery he might have used to describe the preparation of the Sabbath meal by sacrificing another lamb.

Ablestein stood by the witness chair. He had not moved during Cain's narration. His straight right arm acted as a rest as he leaned close to his client. He coughed as much for his own restored composure as to signal a redirection for his audience.

"What did you do next?" he asked.

"I ran."

"Where?"

"Nowhere."

"For how long did you run?"

"I don't know."

"What happened next?"

"God found me."

"Where?"

"I don't know."

"Did he speak to you?"

"Yes."

"What did he say?"

"He asked the famous question. It's the one reported in print everywhere. It has become a tedious part of a parable. I hate the question. I hate my answer."

"You mean the one where he asked you, 'Where is Abel?' and you responded, 'Am I my brother's keeper?'"

"Yes, of course, that one. There was a roar emanating from the whirlwind. I felt rage for the first time. I thought everything: Why did you put me through this ritual? Why have you engineered this event? I never said these things, and he probably knew I thought them. Suddenly, there was a pressure on my forehead, and he gave me the mark you see on my head. My anger deepened against him. I wanted to curse him, but I was afraid. All of this was his doing. He killed Abel, and he knew he killed Abel. Yes, it was my hand, but he moved that hand and pushed that hand with its blade into dear Abel. He was the murderer, not me."

"God was the murderer?"

Ablestein seemed nervous, as if he felt his defense was slipping away with this premature accusation by Cain. He worried the jury would view Cain as crazy, a man desperate to concoct just any story to escape his punishment.

"Yes. God was the murderer!"

Cain became silent. There was a long pause, so long that the jury began to move, fidget, and murmur. The judge heard the rustling and stirred himself.

"Has the defense completed his examination?" the judge asked.

"Yes, Your Honor. I have no further questions." Abelstein replied.

"Since the day is early, does the prosecution or the defense have any objection to proceeding directly to the summary remarks?" the judge asked.

Both men answered that they would have no objection. The foreman of the jury surveyed the four men and seven women.

All consented. The foreman nodded to the judge so that the summaries could begin.

"Mr. Goncrist, you may commence," said the judge.

"Of course, Your Honor," said Mr. Goncrist.

The lean, clean-shaven, and handsome prosecuting attorney stood in contrast to the short, bearded Ablestein. He looked at the jury, with both hands on the railing of the jury box. He turned away and looked back again at them. He held no paper, as if to say he spoke from the heart. His tailored brown suit and cobalt blue tie decorated him with sartorial sophistication. He was no recruit from the neighborhood. Despite the impeccable professional demeanor, he gave the impression of a relaxed seasoned advocate who knew well what he was doing and what he wanted to say. Many favored him to win the case against a man who would use a belief, perhaps a fantasy, to argue against his own responsibility in the murdering of his brother.

Goncrist started: "Members of the jury, Cain killed his brother. We have heard him say so. Mr. Abrad witnessed the act. Abel is dead. What more is there to say?"

Goncrist paused. He looked at the jury and then at Cain. His gaze then swiveled toward the courtroom audience and back to the jury. His eyes were brown and dark. His eyebrows were thick, cantilevering over the eyes to give his skull its dark recesses. He set a morose cloud over his jury recipients. Each juror had a personal story kept hidden during the course of the trial. The already told tale touched some private part of who each person was, but even they did not know how or what. Whether the prosecutor's words would affect their thinking had been the eternal mystery of trials since Athena weighed in on the first in ancient Athens.

"Abel is dead," Goncrist repeated after the eternal pause, "and his brother is the murderer. We are asked by the defense to believe this brother, this Cain," he leaned forward on the rail to emphasize the name, "was in some way innocent of the crime. Cain took his knife when he heard the kind, empathic, soothing words of his loving Abel and drove its blade into him, leading to the death of a man. Was it Cain's hand? Yes. If his hand had not plunged the knife into Abel, would Abel be alive? Yes. Did anyone else claim that it was God's hand that drove the knife into this gentle soul? No. It was Cain's hand. Remember this, jury. Do not fall into the abstract, imagined, unreal ideas of the defense. Whatever your religious belief, do not let them cloud your correct vision, your logic, your sanity. The man who kills is himself responsible. He cannot pass off his guilt onto any conjecture or belief to which he wants to give the blame.

"For centuries, murderers and criminals wallowed in their psychopathic blame game to escape their crimes. It is always someone else, even the victim, who drove them to commit any act against the rules of the social order. If we are to succumb to their make-believe, we are to assent to the loss of the civil agreement to civilization itself. Civilization disappears when the rules are corrupted for the few. The arguments of the psychopaths, the sophistry, the excuses, and the fantasies cannot replace the rule of law and the agreements we all place on ourselves as the body politic. The world cannot function if its fundamental basis is self-aggrandizement and specious dissipation of responsibility. We cannot let fantasy rule and dispel the full meaning of an onerous act. Cain committed murder. For that he must pay!"

Goncrist walked up and down the proscenium of the court to allow the absorption of his words. His skill at drama was well-known. He accented his words with just the right body action. Never too much.

Goncrist continued: "I implore you, as well," looking back into the eyes of the riveted jurors, "to ignore the mark on Cain's forehead. Much has been made of this so-called sign. The defense claims it is proof that the story of God is true. After all, Cain was lost for a long time. The police could find him nowhere. When he showed up in our town, eager to confess for unaccountable causes, he swore he had been shunned wherever he went because of this mark. Ask yourselves this question: what proof do we have he is telling the truth? Mr. Abrad was too far away to verify that once there was no mark and then, poof, there was. Cain's parents cannot be found. Many years have passed, but not too many for the murderer to be lost from the grip of our laws. Put aside the mark and judge the man!"

Goncrist surprised Ablestein. He seemed out of character when he shouted the last statement.

Someone shouted, "Yes. You are right. You are right."

Everyone turned to see who it was. The jurors seemed uncomfortable and shifted in their seats. The judge banged his gavel.

"Order. I want order in this court. Silence!" He pointed to the woman at the back of the room who he saw shouted. "One more outburst from you and I will permanently evict you. Do you understand?"

The woman nodded as she saw the guards approach her.

The judge turned to Goncrist and motioned for him to approach.

"Contain yourself, Goncrist. You know this is a volatile and emotional case. It would be easy to excite everyone. I'm asking for restraint from you," said the judge.

Goncrist showed a mixture of inner cheer with his outward concurrence to obey. With a scowl from the judge, he promised to end his remarks with no further incitements for the crowd.

He turned to the jury and said, "So put aside the mark." He continued as if nothing had happened. "The mark is no evidence that God indeed took any role in this case. There is no proof whatsoever that the mark was put there by anyone but probably Cain's mother after conceiving and delivering him at birth. It's a mere birthmark if it's anything."

There was a subdued chuckle that could not be located.

Goncrist continued: "The case comes down to whether you believe this man truly spoke to and was influenced by God or this influence, if it did occur, exonerates him for his crime. The first issue cannot be decided by anyone. One has a right to one's conviction, but that is all it can be. There is simply only Cain's word. Why should a man implicate himself by denying his cleverly conceived tale? The second issue is the meat, the essence of what you must put into your deliberations. It is the crucial consideration about which you must decide his innocence or guilt. Note that Cain was not driven to murder by God. He said, himself, he was incited to murder by the gentle words of his brother. His reaction came from years of envy which made him misinterpret Abel's attempt to soothe him. You have seen an impressive psychological presentation of the difference between two men. There has been put before you enough material to show that this jealousy may have led directly to the crime, directly to the murder. Finally, even if Cain's claim that God was displeased with him and God provoked him is true, it was still left up to Cain alone to act or not act upon the meaning of that displeasure. He is a free agent. He cannot say he was only the tool of a gray cloud.

"Members of the jury, convict this man of unprovoked murder. Say to the world that the killing of a brother is a heinous act that should never go unpunished. Dispel any thought that a murderer is motivated by a greater divine power. Place the responsibility of man with man for man. Do not let yourself be seduced by his imaginings, his abstractions. Convict him as he deserves. This is what he deserves!"

Again the room was mute.

Judge Ismael broke the heavy silence by declaring, "Since the prosecution took the better part of an hour, there will be a recess for lunch. The court is adjourned until two o'clock."

Ablestein and Cain left the court arm in arm, pushing oglers and reporters to the side as best they could. Even they were

surprised they made it to the limousine without any major inci-
dent. Photographers were madly snapping pictures as Abelstein
and Cain hid in the vehicle and drove away. Cain was pleased that
his journeys into the world had profited him so well that he could
afford to post bail on himself. As the car made its way to the lawyer's firm, where a private lunch awaited, the thought occurred to
him that God, at least, guaranteed no harm would come to him
in his wanderings while he accumulated his wealth. Without that,
he would certainly have been awaiting the outcome of this trial in
somber confinement.

Once in the offices of Ablestein, Gather, and Fisher, the men
took off their coats and settled into the deep, leather-cushioned
chairs reserved for clients. Plates of pasta salad were brought in.
They attacked their food with an eagerness and hunger brought
on by the emotional turmoil of the trial. After they finished—with
plenty of time remaining before they had to return to court—they
sat together, alone, over coffee, for the first time this day.

Cain spoke first: "What do you think?"

"I think we have a good case and a weak case. My position hasn't
changed since you walked into my office with your desert dress
and began convincing me who you were and what you wanted."

"I want an acquittal. Goncrist went for the position you said was
your greatest concern."

"You mean the idea that man is an independent responsible
agent? He is on his own because God wound up the clock of
the universe and left all behavior to itself. Since the universe is
independent of God, you are guilty as independent of him as well?"

"Yes, that one. I mean...I know it's a matter of theology, or, at
least, a matter of interpretation, but the argument does divide the
situation quite well. All of this strikes me as strange. Here I am
asking the jury to believe the truth, but the truth in my case is best
set forth as a theological abstraction. The abstraction can either
be believed or not. It cannot be proved. Oddly, it is the abstraction

that is really true. My story is what truly happened. Goncrist is telling the jury to deny theology because theology can't be real."

Cain put his head in his hands. Ablestein thought Cain was going to cry again, but he didn't. He was only frustrated.

"That's an interesting way to look at matters, Cain, but it's irrelevant to your case. Your conviction or acquittal depends on the jury understanding the special relationship between you and God. The jury must be led to understand that you began that fateful day well-motivated to please. You saw the sunrise possessed with the love of God. You felt no animosity toward anyone, least of all Abel."

"That's true. It's most important to emphasize that."

"Right, and I shall. The main thing to say is that the entire scenario was engineered by an all-powerful being. You were the slave to his will. Even more significant is the fact that he provoked you."

"Provoked me?"

"Yes, don't you see? God had a choice. He could either accept your gift or not. There was no logic to why he rejected you. From our story, anyone can see you tried your best to please him. Harvesting the fresh fruits, pushing the cart up the steep hill, and waiting patiently for his blessing were all indications of your devotion and humility before the Lord. Certainly, you were not motivated by criminal intent then. You wanted to hurt no one or anything. Once God rejected you, rejected you in the absence of any logic I might add, matters changed. His rejection was that of the all-powerful, almighty being he was. You were immediately terrified of the meaning of this, to what it might lead. Hmm, this coffee is hot."

Ablestein had a habit of interrupting himself at the most meaningful moments. It was frustrating to anyone listening.

He continued, back in context: "You made this state of affairs beautifully clear in your testimony. God, then, put you into a new state of mind. After all, you asked yourself—just as you said in court—why did God accept Abel and reject you? Were you being toyed with, a mere test case, a guinea pig? When you killed Abel in your rage, your anger was not directed to your brother, but to God. Abel was God's creation as was your anger. The two of you were ineluctably bound: the active and the passive, the attacker and the attacked. Whether God meant for these events to be a parable or lesson for others is not clear. The result was death for Abel. You did not kill Abel…God did."

Cain sat upright.

"Will the jury accept the proposition that God played the causal role in my story?" Cain asked.

"I have to convince them. We do have Abrad's testimony. He did see Abel bring a lamb to the top of the hill. He did see you push your cart of fruits and vegetables up just after. Mr. Abrad described, of his own volition, the gray cloud over both of you. Best of all, he could not explain where the sheep and the cart went as they separately disappeared following each offering. Goncrist did not cross-examine Abrad because he hoped the issue could be made less important by ignoring it. You can be sure I will make the most of Abrad's words. It is on the record. Even if Abrad did not hear the voice of God and did not witness the miracles, he saw enough. He is key to your defense. Once it is established in the jury's mind that there may be a chance—even a small chance—of God acting in this situation, your acquittal is more assured. Then the defense is that God made it all happen. He rejected you. He inflamed you. He left you bereft and frightened for no ostensible reason that you could surmise. God did all but lift your knife-possessed hand, and he might have done that as well. You killed your brother, my friend, but you are innocent. If anyone or anything is truly guilty in this case, it is not you. It is God. He has inflicted this crime as a story and burden for all mankind. He alone is responsible for the consequences. I will do all I can to prevent him from passing this sense of sibling responsibility and criminal act onto humanity. I won't let him. It shall not be!"

Silence settled in the room for a long time. The two men finished their coffee with the few accompanying cookies. Then, again wordless, they stood to put on their coats. They wanted to have time to return to court by two o'clock.

As they exited the richly furnished offices, Cain turned to Ablestein and said, "Do you think we will win?"

Ablestein looked at him seriously and replied, "You never know until the jury gives the verdict. Once I've given my summary, it's in their hands. We can only hope."

WHY YOU SHOULDN'T CUT OFF MY HEAD

An Ethical Argument against a Terrorist Act
(A Presentation Given at the Columbia University Ethics Seminar)

I am much honored to be here this evening to give a talk on some of my ideas regarding terrorism in general and decapitation in particular. Though it is considered by all rhetoricians a no-no to apologize before a speech, I feel provisos are in order, and I hope experienced speakers in this audience will indulge me. Because I'm aware that many of you are professional philosophers, people who practice and teach philosophy on a daily basis, of you, I beg forgiveness. I am a practicing psychiatrist with the expected deep interest in human behavior. I am not a practicing philosopher. Over the past years, however, like many of you, I have felt it almost imperative that I search for a philosophical justification that would inhibit a reasonable human being from decapitating another. In that quest, I present the following. I do draw from philosophy as an amateur, albeit a very avid amateur, and hope that my references do not cause too much wincing and inward groaning. I look forward to your expert comments and corrections, if deserved, at the end of this talk.

When pondering the question of how to argue with a decapitator so that he does not take action against us, the question immediately arises whether we are dealing with a reasonable human being in the first place. In a sentence, what is our terrorist captor like? Marc Sageman, a CIA case officer in Afghanistan between 1987–89—now retired, also a forensic psychiatrist and author of *Understanding Terror Networks*—wrote a piece for the Foreign Policy Research Institute. This article concerned 400 terrorists from whom he collected biographical information. It was his opinion, based on this investigation, that the vast majority—90 percent—came from caring, intact families. Sixty-three percent had gone to college. (He compared this with the 5–6 percent which came from third world countries). These were the best and brightest of their societies in many ways. Jihadists were overwhelmingly educated in sciences and engineering; few receiving religious or humanities education. Far from having no family or job responsibilities, 73 percent were married and the vast majority had children. There was little or no mental illness as defined by the usual standards in these men. It was his contention that these terrorists were as healthy as the general population. Ten percent of the terrorists in his sample were converts to Islam from Christianity. Also, 70 percent were expatriates. They were "the best and the brightest" sent abroad to study. He, however, found them to be homesick, lonely, and marginalized people who sought out comforting companions, primarily at mosques. They tended to move in together, enhancing feelings of collective identity. (From Parapundit.com, November 23, 2004, Tuesday).

The portrait of our decapitator can either be that of Dr. Sageman's, who described the men in his investigation as well-educated, seemingly normal, and disenfranchised persons who became terrorists by seeking camaraderie or it may fit another profile, such as that of the roughened and onetime-jailed madras educated from a third world country. There is also the fundamentally criminal element that works its way into any destabilized situation. We know our composite is likely to be inaccurate, but no portrait is going to achieve more than that obtained by closely studying a particular individual whose history is well-known. We are therefore forced to create our own protagonist. For our purposes, permit us to assume a useful literary configuration. Our decapitator will be a sane man, but a passionate one. Since the nature of this man's mind is elusive to us who find his violence abhorrent and nearly incomprehensible, we must put aside this sense of disgust at the disparate mental state we are forced to witness and allow that our decapitator is reasonable enough, with a burning need to make a political statement using a public murder or beheading. He may be quite unlike the recently sentenced, rageful, and blustery Zacarias Moussaoui, who was, in fact, not the reported schizophrenic he was suggested to be, but was an abused, maladaptive man barely emerging from an abhorrent childhood. No, our man is somber; he deeply wants the world to realize the unacceptable behavior of his enemy, in this case the invaders of Iraq, and he is calculatedly determined to affect world events. He feels his tools are suicide bombings, roadside ambushes, high-profile kidnappings, and, as in our example, beheadings. He has a strange immunity to the sufferings of his captives, but he is a bit curious about them. He will admit to a certain pleasure in feeling dominant over the creature of the moment and the outward symbolism demonstrated, that being an expression against American and British hegemony. He knows his actions are followed. He knows if he releases his captives he will gain something, but he has a deep conviction that if he beheads them he will gain more. This is his opinion. He is aware that there has been a long tradition of beheadings for political and psychological reasons in the history of Islam and in Christianity. (We may remind ourselves that Shakespeare incorporates the use of heads on pikes in his history plays regarding the Wars of the Roses). He sees the Western horror of beheadings as an advantage to him—a fact that allows his intent have an impact it would not otherwise have. Perhaps he is, in fact, more of a gangster than a thinker, but for this demonstration, if you will allow, he will be given a certain degree of reflective wisdom.

It is convenient to create a story, a pseudo-documentary, to watch in our mind's eye. It will be necessary to go into and out of the story to make certain points. I crave your indulgence for this exercise as it is hoped that the fiction will add verisimilitude to life's sad realities and lend weight to the philosophical points to be made. After all, was there truly a Platonic cave with shadows?

To begin, imagine this scene from your nightmares. It opens onto an undecorated room constructed of damaged cement block. It is part of a larger building partly demolished by American bombs, the bombs of the insurgents' enemy. The windows are covered with boards to block out the light, but bars can be seen over them as well, preventing any escape. Our victim has been removed from a larger room where he has been kept for days. He leaves his three blindfolded compatriots awaiting their fates. He doesn't exactly know what is coming, but he has worried about this moment throughout his captivity. From the time he was picked up in the supposedly safe Green Zone in Baghdad, he has tried to occupy himself with the pressing details of his captivity, but the unavoidable thought that these may be his last days on earth cannot escape him. He only tries to think of the raw specifics about himself, the dirt contours of the floor visible to him since his blindfold had been removed, the names of the men who were jailed with him, or the roughness of his captor as he is dragged away. His hands are bound loosely, but firmly, in front of him. There are shackles on his legs that force him to walk with a necessary shuffle. He is now

seated on a plain wooden chair, forced upon it by two of his cap-
tors who clearly obey the man standing directly in front of him.

"Sit!" Abd al-Qaadir commands.

He is already seated. The light about him seems to have intensi-
fied. He adjusts to see the man before him.

His interrogator, who will also be his future decapitator, stands,
threatening in the view allowed. Three men with machine guns and
grenades on their belts are standing menacingly against a wall. All
have beards. The interrogator is unarmed but roughly dressed in
jeans, shirt, jacket, and kaffiyeh. The victim is welcomed by name
and is gently told of his family who has written about his capture. The
decapitator refers to his work in Iraq. While these niceties are being
uttered, two new men come in with a large and surprisingly modern
TV camera. Since there are no cables, it is clear that it has batteries
and taping abilities. The victim reacts to the presence of the camera.

"It is our little TV show, Carl. We are going to ask you questions
for your Americans," Abd al-Qaadir says.

"No. I don't think so," he blurts out this terrifying realization.
"I think you are going to cut off my head while filming it."

Carl is surprised by his own self-revelation coming from within.
He is even more surprised that his voice is loud and determined.

Abd al-Qaadir stands with his feet spread and stares down with
a slightly smiling face, saying, "Yes, you are right. It is time for you
to die."

The victim shrivels and nearly cries. He shakes a bit, pulling at
his bonds in a desperate unconscious attempt to escape.

"There is no need for you to struggle. Even if you undid the
shackles, you would not get twenty paces before being gunned
down," says Abd al-Qaadir.

Carl feels desperate. As he hears these words, he feels helpless
and does not know what to do. He doesn't want to die, but he also
does not merely want to pee in his pants as an animal reaction.
He thinks of his son in Seattle and his wife. His own father once

bragged to a lawyer friend that his son could talk his way out of anything. He remembers hearing this conversation and being proud. He remembers it inspiring him to join the debating society. He once won an award, capitalizing on his father's pride. He now wants to try something, anything. His chances are slim. He loved philosophy. He knows something about it. He considers his options. Could he actually talk to this man? Try? Is there anything else to do?

"Is it possible to discuss this? What if I can convince you that you should not cut off my head? Would you listen?" Carl asks.

"Listen to what? Your whining? Your cowardly moanings? There is nothing for you to say that can change our passion for this jihad. You are a pawn in all this; you are simply nothing. Your country always refuses to negotiate. As big as it is—with all its tanks, night goggles, and bombs—it cannot stop our jihad, and neither can you," answers Abd al-Qaadir.

"I don't want to stop your jihad. I want to save my life. You are going to cut off my head no matter what, it seems." He fights back his tears. "Give me a chance. I am nothing. Give me a chance. I have things to say that can change your mind. Allow me a few moments. If only you would listen!"

He nearly cries this out. He can no longer stop the tears which flow in spite of himself.

Abd al-Qaadir is bemused. He is in no hurry. The others stand with the camera equipment chittering with humor as if they have seen this before. They have nothing else to do. It is midafternoon. A beheading takes maybe twenty minutes. Unlike his men, Abd al-Qaadir thinks about his unusual victim. Those he beheaded in the past only cried, squirmed, urinated, and defecated. No one had ever spoken like this when confronted with the inevitable.

"You think you can talk me out of this execution. You even have the self-control to argue with me. You think I'm a stupid, a mere madras-educated Sunni, eh? I know more than you realize. You think I am a pig?!"

"You are not a pig. You are my executioner. You hold life and death over me. I only ask you give me a chance to show you the wrongness of this act to me and to anyone else. It is wrong to behead an innocent man. Its consequences go beyond this room."

"Consequences beyond this room?" Abd al-Qaadir spits on the floor in disgust as if the comment made was a kind of sacrilege. "Are you a fool? Of course, the consequences go beyond the room. This is what I expect. This is what I want. This is what all of us want." He then regains his posture and stares at his captive. "It is amazing how calm you are. Very well."

He motions to the others in the room to leave. This is to be a private argument. The other five men grumble in Arabic. He shouts back at them and they leave. Apparently, they have understood nothing of what has transpired, knowing no English. They are cowered by Abd al-Qaadir, and they leave.

"I warn you," Abd al-Qaadir directs a now stern gaze at Carl, "I have little patience for stupidity. What do you want to say?"

The victim sits with his hands still bound in front of him. His muscles relax slightly. He breathes deeply.

"Decapitating me is wrong, but it will take a little time to explain. First of all, the idea of wrong is not a simple idea."

"What do you mean 'not a simple idea'? Don't you mean that wrong is arbitrary? You think I don't realize that you Western dogs think we make up our own rules. Your Western philosopher, David Hume, said that no 'is' implies an 'ought.' You want me to follow this man who never read the Koran?"

This comment was shocking coming from a decapitator who spends his life killing unknown innocents. Carl simply couldn't believe he would know such philosophy.

"Are you saying that since there is no 'ought' which can be defended by the West, there is no morality and no set of rules that satisfy Western and Eastern concerns?"

"I'm saying that in my world we have the morality of the Koran. It supersedes any other philosophy in your world. It was given by God to the prophet, and the 'is' in our world is absolute and not open to question. Your philosopher, Hume, is wrong because he does not know the Koran. It is simple."

"So, I'm to die because you feel that the Koran says that I should or because you are arbitrary and afraid to face the full meaning of Hume's words that there is no absolute morality, yours being no better than any other?"

"The other side of Hume's assertion is that you should die because you are in a war-torn city where your values are not established and there is no reason for you not to die."

"If we put aside Hume for a moment, I would point out to you that Immanuel Kant might have argued, up to a point short of allowing wanton murder, similar to the way you do. He believed in an imperative morality coming directly from human reason. Behavior was demanded by reason of what is right. But you would have parted company to think that decapitating me would be a universal principle on which you could decapitate anybody. Kant, always sensitive to the importance of the dignity of a human being, also stated that a principle applied should be judged by its universality: 'Act only in accordance with that maxim through which you can at the same time will that it become a universal law.' If I'm decapitated, then it would be right for you to be decapitated. Where would you draw the line? Who should and shouldn't be decapitated? What are the rules for who should get it?

Carl watches his executioner ponder the last comment. He doesn't feel he is winning; he isn't sensing safety, but he is allowed to speak. He feels as if he has slightly penetrated the jihad confidence of Abd al-Qaadir.

"What's more important for me is does the Koran explicitly say your enemy should be decapitated as an example to effect change? I think not. It actually says, 'Whoever killed a human being, except as punishment for murder or other villainy in the land, shall be regarded as having killed all mankind.'"

"Yes. The Americans, the British, and the people you work for have promoted 'villainy in the land' and more. God revealed his will to the angels, saying: 'I shall be with you. Give courage to the believers. I shall cast terror into the hearts of the infidels. Strike off their heads, strike off the very tips of their fingers' (Koran 8:12). Also consider, 'When you meet the unbelievers in the battlefield strike off their heads' (Koran 47:4).

"But I am NOT your enemy!" Carl cried out, "I'm just here to work for your country, to help. I'm earning a small living by coming here. I'm not the 'unbeliever in the battlefield.' I'm merely middle management in a company that came to restore the water supply in devastated areas."

"Halliburton. Yes. We know what you do. You are part of the enemy. You came with them for the spoils. You are confused, my friend. You are guiltier than you know."

The victim looks glum, even more so than before. His decapitator is no ordinary thug. He is well-versed in Western and Koranic philosophy. It is easy to see how Carl, Halliburton, and the United States could be lumped together. From Abd al-Qaadir's perspective, he is part of the enemy; he is no different. He is beginning to feel the terror, the sweating, and the instinct to run without being able to run.

"So the friend of your enemy is your enemy. There is no exception. That is why I am going to die?"

"You are not only the friend of my enemy, but you are also my enemy. It is of the greatest good to kill you because you provide a demonstration of those who would desecrate our temples and defile our beliefs, but your death protects us from future do-gooders."

"You can argue that decapitating me will do the greatest good for your followers, but it then follows that others cutting off your head would do 'good' for their followers. Bentham argued the greatest good for the greatest number, but it has been shown that it can create a world where no living is possible for the individual. The effect of this approach is each side argues the Benthamite view, but it's an argument without substance. It is unclear who, if anyone, would benefit from using the beheading approach as an asset. If all feared their heads being chopped off, how could anyone enter into a controversy with you? How could anyone have civil discourse with you? It could be counterargued that eliminating you would do the greatest good, but that would not respect your cause or your religion. It's clear that Bentham's approach leads to a muddle."

"You have come to Iraq to die?" This is a question in a surprisingly soft and mellow tone.

"I came to work. I came to take advantage of a situation in which my work will be rewarded."

"You invade Islam behind the tanks and the military. As they march into Islam, you march behind them in the hundreds to make money off the misery of those who hold the Koran sacred. You contaminate my religion, my culture, and my people. I don't want you here. Your country supports Israel that destroys Palestinian culture. You are your country. Both are one and the same. You must die."

"You surely know I have no wish to destroy you, your religion, or your country. I have no wish to contaminate your culture. I am here to restore the water supplies to Iraq. I plan to leave. Why do you insist on associating my presence with all the political ideas and beliefs of my country? Are you an Iraqi? No. You are Jordanian or Palestinian. Are you fighting for Islam or for yourself? If you cannot dissociate me from my country of 300 million people, why do you ask me to separate you from the Shiites, the Palestinians, or the moderate Islamists? Are you all the same? Should we lump you together or try to understand your unique qualities?"

Both men paused and looked at one another.

Carl felt a slight advantage. He was—for a brief, crazy moment—inspired and emboldened.

"There is no morality in you here. It is your whim, your fancy, to kill me. There is no right or wrong in it; however, you might rationalize that it furthers the cause of the jihad. It is still the impulse of the moment, and it stands for no principle. But there is a morality against it," Carl said.

A smile comes again to the lips of the executioner. It is an almost gentle acknowledgment that the man sitting in the chair before him deserves respect. He still plans to kill him, and soon, but he wants to hear a little more of what he has to say.

"You are aware there are other cultures. You rage against the Christian world, but there are also the Chinese, Indian, and Oceanic worlds. There are hundreds of smaller cultural units: Inuit Eskimos, New Guinea natives, the Montagnard of Vietnam, and hundreds more. Do you plan to kill them all? Do you want to invade them and convert them to your brand of Islam?

At this, Abd al-Qaadir looks irritated. He cannot deal with this question. He has blocked out of his mind anything other than Christianity as represented by Western Europe, and the United States is his only enemy. Besides the Shiites, these crude arrogant Westerners are the only people he thought to conquer.

"Don't give me an anthropology lecture, my friend," says Abd al-Qaadir.

The victim knows the use of "friend" means his time could be very near.

Abd al-Qaadir continues: "Our lands have been invaded. You put the Jewish curse onto our children. You corrupt our teachings. These other people you mention have done none of this. They are not of our concern. If necessary, we will deal with them at another time. This is no argument. I will call my men back. You are wasting my time."

"No. No. Wait. I didn't mention these people for that reason. Each of these cultures has a different morality. How are you to know you have the right one?"

Imagine two philosophers have been observing this dialogue. Each holds a cup of Starbucks coffee. They're watching from a parallel universe through a wormhole in space, but the philosophy being used is well-known to them. They cannot control themselves any further. They know they cannot be heard. It is their private dialogue. They interrupt our story for a moment.

"Whoa! He's a goner. He's going to die," the one with the mochaccino, Professor Feeling, says to Professor Thought."

"What do you mean? He's just warming up. He's about to move into relativism in morality. Can't you see that, Professor Feeling?"

Professor Feeling can hardly contain himself: "This Abd al-Qaadir guy is not going to listen to a long-winded postmodernism dissertation on moral relativism. He's just going chop Carl's head off and be done with it. Besides he has already denied the importance of the Hobbesian contractual perspective while confirming the Hobbesian sense of the brutishness in the lawless expression of power. He states that there is no law, not even a submission of the weak to the powerful, dictated by Koranic text as he interprets it. He is the law, and if he wants to chop this man's head off, there is no implicit agreement between the weak and the powerful to prevent it. Any form of moral relativism demands some kind of contract. He denies there should even be one. He is the contract—whenever it suits his purpose, he'll cut somebody's head off. He is the arbitrary ruler in his kingdom of this building, the domain protected by his henchmen. He is the leviathan of the moment over the individual without agreement—not for the good of anybody but a social structure he creates in his mind. No, he is power because he can't see beyond power. From his perspective, he stops with Hobbes's comment on the lawless nature that exists without a social agreement which I quote in part: "And which is worst of all, continual fear and danger of violent death; and the life of man, solitary poor, nasty, brutish, and short." With this guy, we are in the raw brutish nature of which Hobbes speaks. *He* needs a leviathan like Saddam Hussein to contain *him*. What say you of that, Professor Thought?"

"Do you have a minute? Do you really want to know?"

"Yeah, why not?"

Professor Thought takes a swig of his double espresso and proceeds to expound: "It is very clear by now that the human being is capable of severe atrocities and wonderful moments of altruism. Most of the time, mankind and womankind are in balanced states, expressing neither too much aggression nor a great deal of generosity. Hobbes simplified human nature by seeing it as strongly inclined toward the brutal and destructive. The social contract was to act as a constraint between these observed harsh inclinations, with the Leviathan charged with maintaining the balance of forces in the societal lump. The contract was to give the leviathan the agreement from the common lot to especially dampen the painful destructiveness he felt was inherent in everyone. Locke took an opposing view with the emphasis on humanity's inclination toward goodness. For Locke, you elect a ruler; for Hobbes, you submit to one. Neither was right. Abd al-Qaadir represents mankind run amok. Mother Theresa represents womankind at the extremes of self-sacrifice. We now know that the brain of the human has an amygdala (a bundle of nerves in the temporal lobe) that, when stimulated, can cause rage behavior. The leviathan of the brain, however, is the frontal lobes, the arena of executive functioning. It is very much affected by developmental experiences. With proper nurturing, the frontal cortex can dampen and control the aggressive impulses of the amygdala. In a completely normal, well-brought up individual, however, the amygdala can be stimulated with implanted electrodes, and the otherwise well-behaved person can become enraged. This has been shown in humans and monkeys. So the brain brings into life the summation of the culture as represented by the parents during development as well as the biological, via genetics, allowing the human disposition to balance all emotional forces with interacting neuronal tissue. It is an easy observation that the vast majority of human beings live in a cooperative fashion under laws. The fact that there are malevolent individuals who gather power and overwhelm the vast majority is not an argument against this empirical observation. Although in every culture there is war, murder, and other social ills requiring rules to contain these behaviors, for the most part, the rules for stability prevail, the wishes to raise children to adulthood prevail, and the general hopes to live without war or mayhem prevail as the predominant human inclination. So the brain, as it is genetically composed, has the ability to go into either the mayhem of amygdaloid aggression and madness or follow docile directions. It's most predominant observable state is to contain aggression and to be more or less docile. The result is in societies abhorring murder, writing laws against it, and living in agreement with the rules it creates. This also means that the rules, mostly designed to insure through various routes the sustenance and maturation of the young and the integrated strength of an extant social structure, are somewhat different in their formulation in different cultures. It would appear on the surface that this brain inclination gives a certain moral relativism, but, in fact, the human brain gives a representation of the cultural variation with regards to the inherent biological diversity of itself and its developmental experience."

"My goodness, Professor Thought, what's your point? I can't see the forest for the trees."

He takes a moment to look around. His mochaccino has finished, and he wants another. The Starbucks line, however, is too long, but he decides to wait.

"My point is any ethic has to take into consideration the biological makeup of human kind and has to take, as its starting points, the observable inclinations for the vast majority. Just as the etholo-gist goes into the field to determine the behaviors of animals in their natural habitat and to deduce those animals' biologically determined inclinations, the same must be done for humans. This ethological operation will give a closer approximation of the nat-ural or usual ethics (desirable behaviors) of humanity than trying to defend a particular ethical position."

Professor Feeling suddenly feels he understands. He asks, "Are you saying that ethics could be a kind of reduced observational empiricism beyond philosophical nonempirical attempts to find the absolute in morality?"

"Well said, Professor Feeling. I don't think there is any defense for an absolute ethical position because right and wrong have no existence beyond human language. Raw nature clearly does not have a right or wrong. It simply is. Darwinism implies that it is right to reproduce and maintain the species, but even that is presump-tive. It may be that the life of nature simply exists, and there is no ethic that can be applied to it. A chimpanzee that kills another for food is simply doing that. It is neither wrong nor right for the chimp to kill and eat his brother. It is part of the brain possibil-ity of the chimp that, at the time of the murder of his own kind, experienced hunger. That doesn't mean right and wrong are not important or even defensible. They simply cannot exist as a prefer-ence outside of the nature of the biological-social culture in which they are operational."

"Does that mean there is no right? There is no way to create an argument to defend against this Abd al-Qaadir cutting off this man's head?"

"Actually, there is no absolute argument (any argument which would exist beyond human contestation). Donald Palmer (1991) said, "I believe...that a kind of moral pluralism is required. We should not feel the quest must be guided by only one principle... Rather, we should develop some system of 'moral mapping.'"

There is an argument that is somewhat convincing, and I wonder if our poor fellow will use it.

"Wow, Professor Thought. You always amaze me, even when you're wrong."

"Why am I wrong, Professor Feeling?"

"The decapitator is evil. It's as simple as that. He is beyond the pale. He extends his sword as does no one in any other culture and wants to kill an innocent man."

Professor Thought glowers at this passionate conclusion and feels resigned to go no further. What could he say to something said with such conviction?

So the two philosophers seat back in cushioned chairs, now silent in their parallel universe. They peer over the walls of Carl's decrepit room to listen in and observe, holding new magically filled cups of Starbucks double espresso and mochaccino.

Abd al-Qaadir says, "What do you mean how do I know I have the right one?"

"If all these cultures have a different morality, how do you determine yours is correct? I mean, why or how is it right to cut off my head?"

"It isn't a matter of whether it is right or not. It is what must be done for the jihad. This makes it right."

"Is it practical?"

"Yes, it is practical. You American pragmatists always look at the efficient, the useful. William James has dead for nearly a hundred years, yet he still contaminates your thinking. I will talk American. I will be a pragmatist: I will cut off your head. My fellow jihadists feel the surge of satisfaction that another American is slain. Your country is weakened. My comrades feel the weakness of your nation with its tanks, its guns, and its missiles. We unite to stand before your arrogant weak country which cannot even save one of its citizens."

"What will happen when the jihad is over? How will you deal with America? Great Britain, even Australia?"

"We will destroy the West. The jihad will wipe out the infidels."

"So, you're idea is the entire West will be eliminated, and you will never have to deal with it again? Even if that's true, what about China and India? Their view of Islam will be that your belief on which it is based is excessively threatening. They will not look kindly on your jihad. What will you do with them?"

"We will live peacefully with them. We will have our Palestine, our Jerusalem. They can have their world and we will have ours."

"Will you have trade with them? Will you have diplomatic relations with them?"

"Yes, that is the plan."

"Why should they trust you? Why should they think you will not cut off the heads of their diplomats, their people, and their representatives who think they can travel peacefully to your lands? Why should they think that you will not act capriciously to show your might, to give them the same shame you have given to the United States. Your cutting off my head, your unwillingness to live by any international rules but those you create, makes you lawless and unpredictable. These other nations will not be able to trust you. They will not be able to have trade with you. They will not be able to enter into agreements with you. You have set a precedent that dissolves any people from ever trusting you or wanting to deal with you in any form. Into the future and all memorable history you will be known as wild, murderous Islamists who have no sense of communality and who discourse only with murder, suicidal bombings, and unreasoned attacks. You murdered that innocent woman Margaret Hassan who worked only for the good of Iraqi Muslims for years. The signal you gave was that no amount of decency could be expected of you. You don't think this will influence governments in the future to avoid dealing with you and merely as an outlaw decapitator, not someone with whom they can negotiate contracts."

"Margaret Hassan was murdered by others. I spoke out against it."

"Well, there's a lot of confusion about this in the Western mind. Many think you did it. If you didn't, they think you inspired it. Don't you see where this beheading thing is going? It is repulsive. It accomplishes nothing besides pleasing you and your like. It sets up an atmosphere of distrust which renders future negotiations nearly impossible. It satisfies your personal need for power, but it cannot be justified by the Islamic code, except by your unusual interpretation of the Koran. I am not as wonderful as Mrs. Hassan, but I am no less innocent. I plead with you to realize that no people can coexist on a planet where mutually agreed upon law does not hold sway. Your act is lawless and destructive to both local and international coop-eration. After this is all over, if you are victorious, there is nowhere for you to go. You have to become isolated (restricted)—a prisoner in your own culture. You will suffer from international trade limita-tions from the lack of desire of other people to work with you. But, I repeat. You are not wrong because there is a fundamental law. You are not wrong. You are not right. You are simply operating out of the range of normal human intercourse. Your people with suffer for this and you will not win, even if you win."

"Well, Professor Thought, what do you think? Do you think he will die? Do you think Abd al-Qaadir will cut off the guy's head and send his body to the Americans?" Professor Feeling asks, "Frankly, I think he will very soon be dead."

"Professor Feeling, you may be right. I can't imagine a thug like Abd al-Qaadir being responsive to the 'let's cooperate because you won't have cooperation if you don't' argument posed. I will, how-ever, give credit to our guy. He has remained reasonable in the face of terrible fear. He has argued well. He has not conjured up his own absolute morality, and he really did not play the morality-is-relative card. I think his neo-Lockian contractual position has a lot of viability, even though it shifts the argument away from the traditional social contract."

"What do you mean, Professor Thought?"

"I will tell you. The social contract comes from an agreement between the protected and the leviathan, the powerful and the weak. Our Carl is suggesting something different. He is saying that in the usual ethical intercourse, there is nothing more than an agreement among equals and a kind of consensual shaking of hands. Carl's idea is a not-too-veiled form of democratic behavior in which the powerful and weak lose their meaning. It's Jeffersonian really. There's a bill of rights in there. It's not clear if the body politic can coexist peaceably with extreme ethnic diversity and religious differences. Iraq will be the first experiment for this. However, the idea that a people can create some kind of operating behavior to allow all to live within their own personal contexts is something new. I don't know if Abd al-Qaadir really gets it though. If he did, he would have been forced to let Carl live. He must deny the need for law to cut off Carl's head. If he decapitates him, he is announcing anarchy and self-centered generalissimo rule. Then there is only chaos. He and his like won't survive in the long run, but Carl will be long dead. Actually Carl has made a valiant and cogent argument. It may stand in academia, but it's hard to be sure it will float with a decapitator."

Both men take a swig of their different coffees. They look at each other sadly. Both sigh.

Professor Feeling speaks first: "You know, Carl doesn't have a chance. None of this is going to work. He's as good as dead. You can't talk to an extremist rationally. This entire scenario is unbelievable. Poor Carl. His desperate arguments are wasted. They may be clever but they are useless."

Professor Feeling slumps in his chair.

"You are right, I fear," Professor Thought answered. Careful reflection, though, makes it clear that the problem is not the mean-spirited and inhuman intent of Abd al-Qaadir. The fact is that there is no objective, logically tight argument in contradiction of any human's behavior against another. Hume started it all, and despite his attempt to find rules that might apply universally, he found a poignant reality in suggesting that ethics has no logic. It is all societal and based on people's willingness to operate under a certain set of rules. Heisenberg and Gödel added strength to this perspective. If there is no reality in the atom beyond the statistical and there is no mathematical position that doesn't demand a higher mathematical position, there is no logic that can satisfy all. There is no ethic applying to all humanity that cannot be challenged by part of that humanity. That is why I offered the biological and ethological argument earlier. At least it's a starting point. It may not be absolute, but it is a means to reason how we might behave in a social setting. Carl's comments, considering the larger social structure's reaction to decapitation, is as good as it gets. There is nothing he can say that's unassailable by the decapitator. If the decapitator is looking for an absolute refutation, Carl will die. I'm afraid you are right."

"Let's see what will happen…" they say together.

The two professors, with Starbuck coffees in hand, stare through their wormhole. They see the room clearly.

Abd al-Qaadir motions his men to return. He looks at Carl with intent. He tells his men to start the cameras. He tells Carl to give his name into the blank, square glass eye that reflects his tattered clothes and weary body. Carl stutters, feels himself shaking, and then does as he's told.

IMMORTALITY

by
Robert D. Martin, MD, FAPM, FACLP
Robert Martin
Bob Martin
Robert Usdinsky
Rachmael Usdinsky
Robert Cohen
Bob Cohen
Bobby
Bob
Me

In truth, the fear of death is nothing but thinking you're wise when you are not, for you think you know what you don't. For no one knows whether death happens to be the greatest of all good for humanity, but people fear it because they're completely convinced it is the greatest of evils. And

173

> *isn't this ignorance, after all, the most shameful kind:*
> *thinking you know what you don't.*

—*Socrates*

I imagine you're in the same position I'm in. You, too, are dying the slow death in your mortality—hedging your bets, thinking through your moves. You don't smoke (or you stopped). You exercise. You drink enough red wine to stock your body with resveratrol. You might even have gone the extra steps as I did. You might have reduced your stress load, loved your wife (studies show good marriages are healthier), remained monogamous and developed lasting bonds with your children. All these and more, designed to foster longevity, give you a heads-up on illness and a chance to consider your life. You can become a philosopher, reflect on what it all means, and ask yourself if you've really been able to pull off the "good life."

Then the truth about mortality takes over: "Hey, I'm going to die. I'm a biological organism on this earth for my limited time, and within that span, I will cease to exist. All memories will be wiped away. My memes will go in about sixty years, my cells in a year or so, but depending on the ground (no cremation for me), my bones might last. When the future archeologists find these bones, they will have no clue they belonged to me—the anchors of my body that held the flesh that was attached to them."

Tell me this is not a strange situation. Today I'm here, conscious, writing this prose largely for myself (to help me think all this through), and tomorrow I'll be dead (gone). I'll be all bones, essentially eaten away by the bacteria currently residing in me.

So, the examined life—that searching, that questing for the good life—is to focus on the living, not dead, being. When Socrates took the hemlock, he was clearly ready to die. In fact, it can be argued that he wanted to die. He was seventy, and he felt "enough already!" At least his death was a political and a social statement. If you think about it, Socrates was a massively important political animal. He was famous. He was in plays. He was talked about. Finally, he was killed by representatives of an entire city. How many of us can search for the good life and see its ending in a spectacular display of public caring and angst? Our family might care, but the world will, at the most, nod and reflect in our direction for a few moments, even a few hours or maybe a few days. That would be it. There is a serious question here. Is it better to seek the good life and die like Socrates or take life as it comes and accept the anonymity of a quiet demise? You've got to give the guy credit; he left us with a story of exhibitionism on a large scale. It was no quiet death in a hospital or even a raucous one on the battlefield—where you lie as a body among many, with a dog tag to identify you if you're lucky.

Then there were the existentialists who struggled with these questions. They decided life was the essence, the meaning one created during existence, and it was each of our jobs to make this essence work. Life was otherwise an absurdity, so some argued, which had its nonsense set aside only by the self-creation of meaning. If each individual did not work to find this meaning, there was none.

Is all this birthing, living, and dying an absurdity? The absurd is the completely irrational—the inexplicable and foolish conclusion. I could write pages on just this meaning. Hell, let's stick to the connotation. When intellectuals speak of the absurd, they tend to mean the extreme deviation from anything that makes sense. So if life is absurd, it simply (there's a laughable word) doesn't make sense. And "sense," what is that?

Even when we try to talk (write) about this, we get hung on the petard of language. We, *Homo sapiens*, are language animals. Our world is language, language, and language. It comes so naturally to us that we forget how much it dictates how we think, how we argue, and how much it affects our sense of the real, the absurd, the physicality, and the emotionality of the world we try to understand. How can we not see Wittgenstein as our guiding light here? He taught us what should have been the obvious: many of our philosophical problems come from issues surrounding language.

Try discussing the good life without language. You laugh. Of course, it's impossible to discuss (a language word) anything without words. I suppose an artist could paint, Lascaux Cave–style, meaning of some sort. The best cartoonist would have trouble discussing the good life without words in the cartoons. But you might argue, language is ambiguous, uncertain; it expresses words based on words applied to experience. You might offer the cybernetic equation Herbert Weiner once gave: $I = M / N$ where $I =$ information, $M =$ message, and $N =$ noise. Every bit of information has noise interfering with the message. Whether it's the child's meaningful game *Telephone* or the ambiguity natural to words, the message is always contaminated to some extent. There is no clean and clear information. The solidity of information always approaches an asymptote. That leads to my favorite idea: truth is always an asymptote—an infinitely small approach to the veridicality, the meaning, the accuracy, and the reality of a proposition or a perception.

Given the conundrum that possessing reality poses—the near impossibility to get it or be sure of it—how can you perceive the reality of the good life? Even as you think you have it with death lurking, you may not. The information on the good life proposition may be untrue. It may be, like Plato's shadows on the cave, a personal chimera, an illusion that comforts us. Suppose the good life is really the bad life (the unfulfilled life, the trivial life), would anyone know?

So, everything is an interpretation approaching the truth but never really getting there. This means we are all in a fog decreasing the meaning of reality. We're always trying to convince ourselves that our sensibility is coherent, but we're always subject to the deceptiveness and seduction of language, leaving aside our natural psychological biases.

Language seems extremely seductive. Just take the wave-particle duality in the atom. The words "wave" and "particle" are English terms that strongly make us think of solidness or something with mass or that impermeable something cohering to itself to remain identifiable. A wave is a phenomenon involving the motion or a measure of a moving thing. We can't imagine waves and particles being interchangeable, but quantum physics tells us they are indeed. Young's double-slit experiment drives us crazy. How can a single particle, an electron, go through a slit and leave a pattern on a photographic paper, indicating it interfered with itself as a wave? The finding is really maddening, but it persists. Clearly, there are experiences at play that are foiling the language we have to explain them. Should this be a surprise? I think not.

We develop during our childhood learning words and their applications to things. This learning is intensely mundane. Mom doesn't say, "Here's a rubber ducky, but it's really made of quarks of string energy cohering into a nucleus surrounded by atoms making up the rubber ducky." No, she says, "Here's a rubber ducky." You, the child, see the ducky as particulate (as an entity, as observable) and as a thing that you touch and fantasize about. You love seeing it float and pop up from beneath the inexplicable stuff called "milky-filmed-with-soap-tub-water." And you learn through thousands of these developments that a thing can be a particle (a substance), can be played with, and can even be tasted, but it's not a complex of energy that translates into waves. When quantum physics presents us with a new idea, our language development recoils at its meaning. The language makes us balk, laugh, and deny what we're seeing or what we're told. Suddenly, the world becomes mysterious, even frightening, and the concept of the good life folds into uncertainty, terrible uncertainty.

What are we talking about? Plato and Aristotle lived at a time when the good life was confined by the boundaries of materiality, a sense that there were human-like gods managing things and that human principles were a reality that might be clarified or satisfactorily explained. Immortality was a possibility. When doubt about this proposition became an issue, Christianity and Islam were invented to cover the doubt. There is nothing like an obsession to cover doubt; religion is certainly, whatever else it may be, obsessive.

Take a look at the current time, the time in which I type all this. The cosmos doesn't make sense. The atom doesn't make sense. Biology doesn't make sense. Humans seem to be the instruments of Gaia (the earth)—part of a solar system and mere complex, organically constructed elements in the life experience. What Aristotelian or Platonic dialogue can deal with this? Even if a philosophically pleasing argument can be constructed regarding Greek balance, social and political engagement, and trusting relationships, what about the degeneration and death factor? How do we include that aside from simply accepting it? Some rationalists may say the good death is like the good life; it should be accepted as part of the human condition, and then the good life should be constructed around it. However, doesn't that beg the question: Who wants to believe in the good life with death menacing at every turn? Frankly, is the good life even possible with the deterioration and discomfort of the dying days as part of it? Is the good life the taking of hemlock before death intervenes? Is this what Socrates was really getting at? Wasn't he saying, "Well, if I must die, I'm going to go out with a narcissistic bang? No whimper for me." This seems the strongest argument ever for suicide at the first sign of the entering demise. We could, of course, then commit the Kevorkian error and kill ourselves off prematurely or unnecessarily. How hard is it, to know that death is inevitable before there are any serious signs of it? I think it's pretty difficult.

The quest for the good life really becomes, even more than Plato meant, the solution to the death question. All life is not merely the contemplation of the meaning of death but the dispelling of the power of this contemplation at ruining the good life.

It is not merely enough to talk about entropy and the dying of everything through energy dissipation. I refuse to accept without a fight the idea Thanatos is a part of life. I mean, I refuse to acknowledge that the obvious has to be the necessity. To see death as an unavoidable phenomenon is not to understand it. Is nature saying she had to put death in the equation for there to be life at all? Why? Explanations abound, but for the contemplative living, they are unsatisfying.

Life, then, appears to be a process whereby organisms of a wide variety go through the act of being born, developing, reproducing, and dying. You cannot refer to life without the dying part. We humans have been given a gift (or a curse) that other organisms do not seem to have. We have consciousness, awareness; we know we're going to die. If I had to invent a more ironic demonic force, I would be hard put to exceed the one of living yet knowing I will be dying. Whether entropy covers the topic or the mystery of an annihilating existence prevails, this realization is very hard to accept. If the earth is a contained globe of vibrating life, why renew its life forms and kill its life-forms in a persistent and unavoidable fashion? I can imagine an earth where life-forms live forever and never have to die. This idea of renewal has been brought to the fervor of religious belief, probably in an attempt to assuage the pain of contemplated extinction, but there is no reason to assume this is necessary. This is what we are given. With consciousness, we do our best to deal with the inevitable and create rationalizations to help us do this. You would think the arduous journey of development with its accumulated knowledge would offset the need to kill off the very living being that this journey was all about.

Okay. So, we have to accept death, and the pursuit of the good life really means searching for the value in the existence we have during the time we have it. The good life doesn't really include the good death since that's the end of things anyway. Let's look at the good life idea, breaking it into sections.

First of all, there is the problem of "good." Values and their meaning are a many fibered nets. Essentially values are human-based. Only humans, with their language, worry about the good, the bad, and the in-between. I'm always impressed by how easily the human-based aspect of values is unappreciated. Whether it's the Ten Commandments or an arcane philosophical discussion of ethics, I find it is usually not the case the argument includes the fact that language and human needs are at the core. There are no values beyond the human. If the earth thinks the carbon dioxide in the atmosphere is bad for its existence, the earth is not express-ing that. If all life dissolved because of global warming, as bad as that seems to us, the earth would have little to say, think, or feel about it. After all, it's a mass that revolves around the sun, just like Mars and Venus. The other planets don't have life. Human values are what give global warming its imperative, not any other value source.

What other value source might there be? If humans believed in a god source, that would be the "absolute" basis for values. Humans, however, would have invented or created this god, and so the source devolves back to them. All desperate searches for abso-lute values fail because the meaning of values falls back on human language and assessments.

"Good" becomes a term couched in the lives or the experi-ences of the people who use it. The good in life is pretty much a bias. If Socrates thought it was an involved citizen who sought wis-dom, this was Socrates's value. If Machiavelli thought it was killing your enemies to sustain your power, that was his. He also thought, by implication, that getting back to Florence was valuable, but he lived his life without this accomplished.

We must argue carefully here. The question doesn't resolve to the notion that all value is relative. Value may be different among different cultures. That is because value is human and contrived by humans for their needs. This is different from saying there is no value because it varies, which is the lament of the cultural relativists. No, value is rather to be viewed as a human construct. Its importance to humans is it provides a framework for social existence. The veridity of the value is limited to the humans who hold it. It's true for them because they constructed it to be true for them. The matter does not come down to all values are different and relative to the tribe or group that espouses them. Values are human needs that are applicable to human concerns.

We then have to see that good is a value that cannot be universalized. The good in the "good life" becomes a construct. This construct can please many, a few, or a single person. Its value or power cannot be absolute, however much it operates to seemingly satisfy the community that espouses it.

All right then; this is interesting, perhaps frustrating, sophistry. What does it mean when you're deteriorating and examining a spent life? What does it mean when you're planning a life for yourself? Say you're in your twenties, and you're talking to a very wise person. You ask them, "What is the good life?" This person answers you. He or she states that the good life is virtue, involvement, financial security, family, and friends. This must be sustained with a balance of needs and with good proportions in all behavior. A sense of the reality of existence, its ultimate loss, and an ability to feel comfort despite the decay that ultimately will befall you are also included. You hear this advice and agree. You decide to follow these precepts as best you can and wish the adviser farewell and a good day.

The problem arises as you try living these precepts and the sufferings of life intervene. A loved one may be lost, you may be treated unjustly by an employer, other people may create conflict for which you're unprepared, or your own health may deteriorate prematurely during a relatively youthful time. Suddenly, you realize the advice was insufficient. There are enough unexpected elements that may make the good life unachievable. The realization reveals that the good life is a value-laden idea immersed in the culture in which it's declared and it is a limited precept in a complex world. In fact, there is no good life; there is only the best life possible. The good life includes this knowledge: life is difficult, painful, uncertain, and unreasonable. This knowledge includes the awareness that allows you to combat the unpleasantness of existence, the uncertainties of tomorrow. This includes the realization that there may be no immortality.

If there is no immortality, is life absurd? That's a value-laden question. We don't know what life is, why it is, why it expires, or what it's supposed to accomplish. What we don't understand can't be viewed as absurd, except as a prejudice—a prejudgment erupting from the culture of our lives. Life simply is, and we are the sentient beings that observe it as best we can. Death is the same. Death simply is, and all metaphors surrounding it are our creation.

There is no life, value, or death beyond our interpretation of these ideas/feelings/perceptions. If some of us want to create a framework called religion to answer these questions, there is no reason to stop them. After all, given the perplexity of these matters, why discourage anyone from explanations to salve the pain of what they signify. Religion may not be an opiate, but it certainly is a comforting structure. There is no surprise that the world of humanity has created many religions struggling to alter the painful realization that life is a terminus event, struggling to explain the observed mysteries of daily living, and struggling to give solace to the question of lost consciousness. Religion is humanity's attempt to explain the inexplicable.

I sit here writing all this for myself. I end with the conclusion I believed in at the beginning—a belief evolving over a reasonably fortunate life of seventy plus years. I see no way out of this situation that feels sad, tragic, and undesired. I'm stuck in the mortality with all other humans, a mortality without explanation. I wait.

AUTHOR BIOGRAPHY

For Robert David Martin, writing has always been one of his main passions. He is a keen observer of the human condition, something his long career as a physician has fostered and developed, and his patients serve as one of his major inspirations as well as the world around him.

When he isn't working or writing, Martin enjoys playing classical piano, listening to chamber music, and spending time with his family. This is his third book.